Contents

Apples and Princesses

Book Two of *The Tales and Princesses Series*

Aleese Hughes

ISBN: 9781088563564

Aleese Hughes

Dedication

For my sister-in-law Emeline, who
will forever be my biggest fan.

Chapter 1

I rubbed my arm, wincing at the pain. The bruise was already starting to form. I clenched my jaw and wiped at the hot tears spilling down my cheeks. My father's abuse didn't make me sad any-more—it made me angry.

I pushed through the trees and ran faster, not knowing where I was going. All I knew was that I just wanted to run. I often found solitude in the woods after a particularly bad bout of temper from Father, but it had just been particularly bad. He struck me more than once, and I didn't know how much more I could take. I was beginning to reach my threshold of tolerance.

My father was a rich lord with a manor in the country, and his land went on for miles, so I had no idea of knowing how far I had to go before I could be free. But did I want to leave? What would I do; where would I go?

Shaking my head, I stopped, staring up at the night sky past the bright green leaves of the forest. The wind chilled me, and I regretted running out into the night wearing only a thin, short-sleeved gown.

"Hello, child."

I jumped at the voice, whirling around to see a ragged old woman with little gray hair left on her head. Her teeth weren't much better. In her arms, she held a large wicker basket full of red apples. The skin of the fruit gleamed underneath the moonlight.

"Who are you?" I squeaked, inching away from the woman.

The woman licked her chapped lips and smiled. "I've been going by Bavmorda lately, and I rather like that name."

Bavmorda started stepping towards me, seemingly desensitized to the sharp branches under her bare feet. I gagged at the sight of her long, yellowed toenails.

"And you, my dear, skin as white as snow, lips the color of blood, hair as black as ebony... You must be Snow White."

I cocked my head, not knowing whether to feel nervous or curious. Magic was a common practice in the Edristan Kingdom, and I had met a few magicians and fortune tellers in the past, but it was not always a respected practice.

"Are you a witch?"

Bavmorda cackled, her throat moving like a croaking toad's. "That's one way to label what I do." She moved even closer. "I've wanted to meet you."

I didn't move away from the woman this time. "Why?"

4

Bavmorda shrugged clumsily, the basket still in her arms. "I have seen that our paths will cross many times in the future."

That made me laugh, and the sound of my voice echoed around us. "Is that so?"

I knew fortune tellers to be more tricksters than to have actual, supernatural foresight. At least, the few that traveled to the Manor for Father's entertainment gave me that impression. The witch knew my name, but anyone could have a lucky guess. Maybe she inquired after the White family before... Or perhaps she knew of White Manor and its inhabitants.

"I know what you're thinking." Bavmorda set the basket down and stretched out her back. I winced at the sound of many joints and bones popping all at once. "Let me prove my abilities to you." She wiggled her knobby fingers and grinned. "Your mother wanted to name you Snow because of your beautiful, fair skin and rather liked how it fit with the surname of 'White.' Unfortunately, your mother died due to complications of your birth, and your father hasn't been the same ever since."

In the blink of an eye, Bavmorda came up to me and grabbed my bruised arm. "Your father's insanity tends to cause you some unwarranted pain, if I'm correct in saying so." She clicked her tongue. "How sad."

I pulled my arm away from the witch's grasp, then immediately regretted the brash movement against my bruises.

"How—"

Bavmorda rolled her dark eyes and sighed. "People always ask me 'how.' I'm a witch, that should be enough explanation."

Despite the woman's unnatural ability of "knowing things," I didn't find myself scared.

"Why all the apples?"

"Oh, those!" Bavmorda looked at her basket in disgust. "I confiscated those from a lowly warlock in town. He thinks it's okay to give out poisoned apples like candy." She put her hands on her hips. "He thinks it's funny."

My curiosity came to its peak.

"Poisoned apples?" I said, moving to touch one.

Bavmorda placed herself in between me and the basket. "What do you think you're doing?"

I crinkled my nose at the witch's pungent breath. "Sorry."

"You shouldn't be playing with these," Bavmorda spat. "*One* bite can put someone into an almost permanent coma. More than that will *kill*."

She pulled her holey shawl back over her shoulders, shivering in the night air and pulled the basket back into her grasp with a grunt.

"Until next time, child."

I watched as the woman hobbled away. Then, out of nowhere, one of the apples rolled from the top and fell onto the forest floor. The witch didn't seem to notice. I waited until Bavmorda was out of sight and rushed to grab it.

I looked at the deep red apple against my white hands and slid my fingernails along the hard skin. It was one of the most delicious-looking apples I had ever seen. My thoughts started turning. I didn't completely believe that someone in town would just be giving out lethal produce. On the other hand, if Bavmorda had been telling the truth, I might be able to get some use out of this apple. I thought of my abusive father. But would I? Would I even be able to follow through with it?

I tucked my hands and the apple away at the front of my purple, silk skirts and closed my eyes. The breeze blew through my dark hair that flowed undone past my hips, and a smile formed on my blood-red lips. There was no harm in trying.

Chapter 2

Princess Dalia Char's life was perfect. She loved being the Princess, she loved her kingdom, and she loved her parents. Nothing could ever get in the way of her wonderful situation. Or so she thought.

Dalia daintily brought one bite after another into her mouth. Her plate of sausage and eggs was delicious. The food was *always* delicious, and she couldn't help but marvel at and appreciate that fact.

"Dalia," King Rory said from the other end of the long table. His bright red hair matched the plush of the chair he sat upon. "Your mother and I are traveling to some of the outlying villages today." He placed a hand lovingly atop Queen Margaret's knee. "We're due for some more public appearances, I think."

Dalia dabbed her lips with a napkin before speaking. "I promised to ride with Lady Aeryn today, Father."

"Oh, that's right," her mother chimed in. The King opened his mouth to protest, but Queen Margaret shot him a playful, warning look. "You have fun today, dear. Don't worry about any duties today."

Dalia smiled prettily at her mother. Queen Margaret smiled back with a twinkle in her green eyes. Dalia received her own green eyes from the Queen but had red hair like the King. She was told, however— especially by her mother— that those two things were a good combination.

"May I be excused?"

The King and Queen nodded, and she bolted from her seat. She rushed over to kiss them each on the cheek. Dalia began to step briskly out of the spacious dining room, heels clicking against the smooth, marble floor.

"We'll expect you to come with us next time!" her father called after her. There was laughter in his voice, and Dalia chuckled herself.

"Of course, Father!"

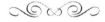

"It's so *hot*!" Aeryn shouted to the trees.

Dalia and her lady-in-waiting rode side-by-side along the hidden dirt path behind the castle. It was the only place the Princess could ride without getting bombarded by townspeople, or even nobles, with a plethora of questions, comments, or just coming by to say, "Hello." Dalia relished in the solitude, and it helped that the trail was beautiful. She loved the bright green leaves and the pretty daisies blooming on every side of them.

"Well, it *is* summertime," the Princess said.

Aeryn groaned, flipping her sweaty, blonde hair out of her face. "I know, but you'd think the shade of the trees would help a *little* bit. It's just so muggy!"

Dalia giggled. Her lady-in-waiting was often negative, but the Princess had always been fond of her, and the company she gave.

"Riding was your idea."

Aeryn stuck out her tongue but was unable to suppress her own laughter.

"Fine," she conceded. "I'll try to enjoy myself. Beat you to the creek!"

And with that, Aeryn clicked her heels against the black flank of her horse and bolted away.

"Hey!" Dalia shouted after her, urging her own horse into a sprint.

The Princess's horse was a magnificent beast with a gleaming, white coat and strong, yet lean, muscles. Her name was Flicker, and she was a young horse with a lot of spirit and was incredibly loyal to Dalia— especially for an animal. And the Princess was just as loyal to her. Dalia caught up to Aeryn quickly and passed the young woman with ease.

"No fair!" Aeryn shouted.

Dalia pulled sharply on her horse's reins when she reached the small creek she and Aeryn often rode to together. The leather of the reins rubbed painfully against her palms, but her triumph was enough to help her ignore it.

"How many wins is that now? One hundred and... twenty?"

Aeryn pulled on her own horse's reins and rolled her gray eyes. "It's just because you have a better horse."

"Princess! Princess!"

Aeryn and Dalia turned their heads sharply to the shouting. A manservant that Dalia vaguely recognized (there were too many staff members to remember faces to names) was riding up to them on his own horse, a much older beast than what the young women were riding. As he pulled in beside them, he gulped for a breath of air. His eyes were wide in shock.

"What is it?" Dalia pressed, cocking her head to the side. Upon closer inspection, she realized he was one of the stable boys. The scrawny one. What was his name...? Robin?

"Your Highness," he breathed, "something has happened."

Chapter 3

"Snow, you wretched child! Where is my dinner?"

Agnes, the head chef of White manor, shut the kitchen doors to muffle Lord White's shouting.

"Your father," the plump woman fumed, "treating you in such a way."

I continued rolling the pie dough I had been working on, sweat cresting on my dark brow.

Agnes walked up to me, raising her own eyebrow. "Pie wasn't on the menu tonight, dear."

A cloud of white flour went into my face as I patted the dough smooth with my hand. I turned away from the food to sneeze.

"I know, but I wanted to surprise Father."

Agnes shook her head, her frizzy, brown curls bouncing off of her chubby cheeks. "You're too good for him, child."

"I don't know if this counts as being 'too good for him,' Agnes. I'm just making an apple pie."

Agnes walked over to the large, stone ovens to my right and pulled out the juicy roast she'd been laboring over that entire day.

"Well, if that be the case, I hope you'll let me

and some of the other kitchen servants have a piece."

"No!" I cried.

The little chef froze with the roast half-way out of the oven.

I scrambled for an excuse. "It's just that this is a *very* special pie for Father. I don't want anyone else touching it."

Agnes shrugged. "If you say so, dear."

After making some finishing touches to the dough, I pulled out a bowl of sliced apples I had hidden under the counter. Among the slices was the apple I stole from the witch the night before. I poured the fruit into the crust, added some juices, and finished it off in preparation for the oven.

"Snow!"

I jumped at the sound of my father's shouts piercing all the way from the dining hall and through our kitchen walls. It was never good when he got angry.

"You'd better take your father's dinner to him," Agnes said, handing me a plate with a tender piece of beef topped with gleaming carrots and potatoes.

I took the plate, then looked to my unfinished pie.

"I'll put the pie in the oven. Now shoo!" Agnes waved me off, getting a little distressed.

I hesitated, but after another shout from my father, I decided to let Agnes take care of the pie. I'd be back before it was cooked, anyway.

Traipsing through the hallways with my shoulders hunched, I found myself shaking. My grip on Father's food was faltering. It was always terrifying to approach my father during one of his tempers, but tonight was critical. If everything went according to plan, Father wouldn't be a problem for me anymore.

The paintings of my various ancestors adorning the side of the halls glared down at me with disdain, as if they knew what I was about to do. I avoided looking at the depiction of my late mother to my left. It was always too painful for me to see the face of the woman I never met. People always said the likeness between Mother and me was uncanny, and they weren't wrong. All except the coloring. She had been much tanner than I. I couldn't help but wonder at what she would think of my situation. What would she think about my father's rage and the... the hitting? Would she approve of what I was about to do?

I shook my head, pursing my lips as I reached the large, swinging doors to the dining hall. Taking a deep breath and straightening my shoulders, I entered.

Rolland White was a large, burly man who intimidated anyone he ever met. But rumors said my mother was the one person to have ever softened his heart. Her death threw him into madness, and he took it out on me more than anything — forcing me to work with the servants, abusing me... He resented me for killing his wife. I knew that because that is what he always told me.

Father was sitting at the head of the long table, back turned to the roaring fire in the hearth. He was picking at the dirt in his fingernails with a small dagger that never left his side. When hitting didn't seem like enough for Father, I was often threatened by that blade. Father's booted feet were placed on top of the table's surface as he lounged back in his chair.

"It's about time, Snow," he said without even looking at me. He ran his fingers through his black hair and groaned. "I am starving."

I lifted my chin up even higher and set the food before him. Before I could even blink, his hand struck the side of my face, and I yelped in pain.

"That's so you won't be as long next time."

I forced myself to stop trembling and stood even straighter than before. I stared at my father as he snarfed down the food like an animal, pieces of beef sticking to his thick beard. There had been many times in my life where I wished for acceptance and love from this man, but all I could feel in that moment was a burning hatred that ate me up inside. Too many bruises and too many cruel words. I was ready for him to die.

"What are you staring at?" he shouted. He inched out of his chair slowly, dagger still in his hand. The blade glinted menacingly from the firelight.

"Father?"

"What is it?"

I looked down to the weapon in his fist, remembering all the moments he threatened me with it. He had never gone as far as to cut me, but it was scary all the same. Many times I thought he might snap and actually use it against me, but that day never came. I pushed down any fear I felt and let my hatred fuel my bravery.

"I made you an apple pie tonight for dessert. I hope that's something you might be interested in trying."

He sank back into the embroidered cushions of his seat, raising an eyebrow at me. "Is that so?"

I nodded.

"Fine," he waved me off. "But bring it quickly! I don't have all night!"

Meaning he wanted to leave as early as he could to the local tavern for a night of gambling, drinking, and women. When he wasn't running his textile business, a successful endeavor that had lasted for generation after generation of Whites, he was getting drunk. That's all he cared about. Money and alcohol.

"It'll take about another half an hour, or so."

He growled, gesturing for me to grab his empty plate. "I'm not leaving for another hour yet. Bring it to me in my study."

I walked away, my steps echoing loudly in the empty room. Agnes and the other servants told me of Mother's love for décor before she died, but I was also told her beautiful furniture and antiques were one of the first things Father got rid of in his grief.

My lip began trembling at the thought of my mother and who she was, wishing I had known her. I shook my head. I needed to focus on the time at hand.

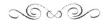

Father's study was where he spent most of his time. Well, if he wasn't drinking at the tavern. Although he did drink a lot in his study, too.

I held a warm plate in my hands with a giant slice of steaming apple pie resting atop it as I knocked at the door. The smell made my mouth water. I hadn't eaten yet, but I was not about to take a bite of a possibly lethal pie. I had been careful to dispose of the rest of it, in fear of an innocent bystander sneaking a taste. The rush of nerves made my legs wobble, but I tried to ignore them and forced my hands to remain still.

"Enter!"

I turned the cold, brass knob with my free hand and carefully stepped around the mess of books, papers, and empty bottles scattered across the room.

"Father," I said, "your pie."

He downed the final drops of a bottle of wine in his grasp and sat up straighter in his chair.

"Put it on my desk." He hiccupped just as soon as he stopped talking.

I pushed aside the piles of papers in front of him, careful not to let any of it hit the floor, and set the plate in front of him.

"Fork?" he spat.

"Oh, I—"

He clumsily waved away my words, too drunk to strike me. "Never mind."

I watched, relieved, as he still picked up the piece, seemingly unaware of the hot glaze dripping onto his hand, and bit into it. I watched in morbid curiosity as he downed bite after bite, finishing the large piece within seconds. Was it really going to work?

My father hiccupped again and darted his eyes around the room, searching for something.

"Do you see any other unopened wine bottles?" He hiccuped a third time.

My shoulders fell, but I wasn't sure if I felt relief or disappointment that the apple didn't work. I knew that the witch had to have been lying, anyway.

Before I could move to find more wine for my father, I heard him begin to gag.

"Father?" I inched closer to him.

He was grabbing at his throat, dark brown eyes bulging dangerously.

"Help," he choked. "Help me."

I stood frozen in place but was surprised to feel my lips begin to twitch in a smile. I immediately felt mortified at my quickness to feel excitement at the poison working.

He looked at me in terror, unable to say another word as his mouth started to foam. His body convulsed violently as he tried to grab at me, knowing I had done something to him. I watched as his shaking slowed, and his limbs begin to relax until his eyes stared emptily to the ceiling.

Chapter 4

I ran. That is all I could do— just run. I had gathered a few travel outfits and a little bit of dried meat and fruit before I gave my father the apple pie, just in case he died.

And he did.

After his death, I grabbed all the money I could find in his pockets and the study and snuck out the back. Most people were asleep by the time I got out.

I didn't know how far I needed to go before the servants learned of my father's demise, and my disappearance, but the fear of getting caught with my crime was enough to make me not want to be there when they did. And then I realized with a sudden feeling of pleasure that this was my chance for a fresh start, and I wasn't going to lose that.

I smiled as I ran, my dark blue cloak billowing behind me. I had expected the guilt of killing my father to overwhelm me, but the thrill of imagining what was to come squashed those feelings. At least in that moment.

Looking behind my shoulder, I couldn't see the looming image of the enormous manor shining with white stone any longer, so I decided it safe to slow down and catch my breath. The sound of crickets and wind whistling in the grass and trees surrounding me was beautiful. The stars glinted above as if winking, and the man in the moon grinned down at me.

Tears of joy began to spill down my face, and I fell to my knees, not caring about the possible grass stains on my brown skirts. I knew I needed to keep going, but I wanted to relish in the moment. Never did I think freedom would come. From birth, I was my father's slave—his unwanted child. He beat me, he cursed me, he hated me. I was his prisoner. And now, I was free.

"You there!"

I leapt up from my position and poised myself, anticipating an assault. A young man, not much older than me, stepped from behind the shadows and approached, small twigs snapping under his black boots. In his left hand, he held a small hatchet and in his right a simple, wooden bow. He shouldered the sheath of arrows on his back and glared at me.

"What is a girl like you doing out here? And so late, might I add?"

I held my protective stance, hand slowly reaching for the blade at my waist. As a last-minute thought, I grabbed Father's dagger from his dead hands. I had no knowledge of how to use such a thing, but having a weapon of some sort put my mind at ease.

"Are you gonna answer me?" he said, pointing his ax at me threateningly.

"I'm a traveler."

He raised an eyebrow. "Where are you going?"

"Wherever I want to go."

He relaxed his hatchet arm, laughing. "That's quite the answer, miss." He leaned back on the broad trunk of the tree directly behind him. "Where are you coming from?"

I squinted my eyes at him, studying his thin face. He didn't seem to want to cause me any real harm, but I wasn't about to tell him anything.

He shrugged. "Whatever. Just be careful. You're right on the border of Lord White's land. He doesn't take kindly to intruders."

I looked behind my shoulder and into the distance. I reached the outside of Father's land? I had never actually gone outside of it— ever.

"How do you know?" I asked. "How do you know that's his land and that he hates intruders?"

The boy smirked at me, dimples forming on his tan cheeks. "I'm a huntsman. Lord White has some of the best game on the entire west side of the Edistran Kingdom. One time, he caught me shooting a deer on his property, and boy, did I get an earful. And some nasty threats, mind you."

That sounded like my father.

"Look, miss," he continued, "I won't hurt you. My name's Nicholas Smith, but people call me Nick."

He inched closer to me and outstretched a

gloved hand. I hesitated, but took it in my own and shook it.

"My name's Snow…" I paused, realizing I shouldn't say the last name, "White."

He cocked his head. "Snow? Just Snow?"

I nodded quickly, pulling my hand away from his.

"Huh." Nick looked down to find where he placed his hatchet, light brown bangs falling into his face. "Well, Snow, if you have nowhere to go, you're welcome to tag along with me. I'll warn ya, though, no comfy beds and porcelain tubs with this guy."

"What do you mean?" I asked.

"I travel all over, never settling in one place. I basically camp out in the woods every night. Once in awhile, I'll catch some good game and sell it for food and lodge, but not often."

Nick sheathed his hatchet's blade and hooked it to his belt. "Last chance. You coming, or not?"

Every instinct I had inside me screamed that it was a bad idea to follow around a strange huntsman, but after really thinking about it, I had never left the White land before in my life. How was I supposed to know where to go and how to fend for myself? I had no plan whatsoever.

"I'm coming," I said.

Chapter 5

Princess Dalia watched herself in the mirror as Aeryn situated the black veil atop her head. The fabric came over her face, hiding the pools of tears in her bright green eyes.

She still couldn't believe it. Her parents were dead. How could something like that happen? It was just a simple carriage ride! How had something so harmless become so deadly in only one day?

"Your red hair really stands out with the black ensemble, Princess."

Dalia tilted her head to the right to look at her fiery curls. "My hair always has a way of standing out at the worst times."

Aeryn smiled, crinkling up her tiny nose. "Don't be silly, Your Highness. It's beautiful."

Dalia sighed, slumping her shoulders. "How am I going to do it, Aeryn?"

"Do what?"

"Be Queen? I'm only eighteen! My parents were supposed to live for *at least* another decade or two!" Dalia placed her face in her hands, trying to keep from sobbing again.

Aeryn gently lifted the Princess back up. "You'll ruin the rouge I just put on your cheeks."

Dalia laughed despite herself. "Sorry."

"Besides, you shouldn't think about that right now. Today is the funeral." Aeryn stepped back to study the Princess.

Dalia took a deep breath. "I think I'm ready."

Dalia stood at the front of the crowd and listened to the priest's words. She stared at the two closed caskets before her, feeling completely numb. No one let her see the bodies, meaning they were too beat up from the accident. She still didn't understand how it happened. Did something scare the horses, driving and rolling them into that ditch? Did a wheel come loose? All they had told her, all they had said to her: it was an accident. An unfortunate, tragic accident.

A tear trickled down her cheek, and she tried to swallow down the lump in her throat.

"Your Highness."

Dalia turned to see Lord Magnus breathing on her shoulder. His face was so close she could see all the wrinkles in his scaly skin. Dalia shivered. She never liked Lord Magnus.

"See me after the ceremony. In my study. We

need to discuss our plans."

She watched as the old man slipped back into the crowd. Leave it to Lord Magnus to ignore the untimely death of a girl's parents *during the funeral* and move right on to the logistics.

It wasn't long before the caskets were placed into the ground and Dalia was directed to throw the first piles of dirt onto her parents' graves. She tried with every bit of strength she had left to stand firm for the people there as she did so, grateful for the black veil obscuring the view of her trembling lips.

Dozens of nobles and subjects wished her their condolences as she tried to leave. She felt smothered by the people and had a hard time breathing.

"There you are, Princess." Aeryn pushed through the masses and grabbed Dalia's arm, squeezing it lovingly.

Dalia smiled. "Thank you," she mouthed to her.

Aeryn led Dalia out of the gravesite and back towards the castle, shooing anyone away that tried to bother them. It took them about ten minutes to traverse the path, longer than average since Dalia was purposely trying to take a longer time in avoidance of her meeting with the royal advisor.

"Lord Magnus wishes to see me."

Aeryn huffed. "Can't that wait?"

Dalia shook her head. "He's right. We need to figure out how and where to go from here."

The two were silent as they entered the castle.

Dalia stared at the red carpet of the halls they followed, trying to keep her mind off of her sorrows.

"We're here," Aeryn said. She gave Dalia a tight hug. "Good luck."

Dalia straightened her shoulders back, moved the veil off of her face, and knocked on Lord Magnus's study door.

"Come in!" he croaked.

Dalia stepped into the room, trying to look regal and queenly. She was going to prove to herself, Lord Magnus, and the rest of the world that she could do this. Her parents would want her to be strong, to be the best queen she could be.

"Princess," he said, moving to stand and bowing his head in respect. "I never gave you my condolences."

He gestured for Dalia to take a seat in front of the large desk that spanned from end to end of an equally large room.

Because you don't care how I feel, Dalia thought.

"Thank you," she said instead.

Lord Magnus sat back down, ancient bones creaking. He rubbed his bald head with his hands, each finger wearing a gaudy ring. Dalia tried not to roll her eyes at the sight. In every way, Lord Magnus always wanted to portray himself as the *best*. Through his manner, dress, speaking...

"We need to discuss the best steps for moving forward, Princess."

"Of course."

"First thing's first, we will crown you as Queen

as soon as possible, but I do think the people will feel more comfortable for you to have a husband, as well."

Dalia gaped at the man. "What?"

Lord Magnus interlocked his skinny fingers together. "You are young. An experienced husband, someone royal, of course, will not only ease the mind of your subjects, but it will help you in many ways."

Dalia couldn't find words.

"Your coronation is in five days. Then a month from now, there will be a ball inviting many kingdoms near us: Mardasia, Polart, and Wilaldan, to name a few. King Alfred of Wilaldan has agreed to the marriage between you and his son Prince Frederik. The ball is where you will meet and announce your engagement."

"Are you serious?"

The Lord raised an eyebrow. "I don't know why I would be joking."

Dalia wrung her hands together. "Is this really the best option?"

Lord Magnus nodded. Though the Lord wasn't the most appealing of men, Dalia trusted him. He had been with her parents from the beginning of their reign as a loyal advisor, and his advice was seldom wrong.

"Alright," Dalia said. "I'll get married."

Chapter 6

I stood in the street, waiting for Nick to finish negotiating with a merchant. He had caught two big, juicy pheasants that morning. One had been our breakfast, and the other he was hoping to get a little money for. I'd been traveling with Nick for a few days, but I still hadn't told him of the few gold, silver, and copper pieces in my satchel. That was something I thought best to keep to myself. I didn't know how long I'd stay in the company of Nick, and I still didn't trust him completely. He hadn't done anything suspicious in the days I'd known him, per se, but it was hard for me to understand why a man would be camping out in the woods for the bulk of his life. It was certainly not something I enjoyed— smelling like fire and sleeping on the hard ground, not knowing if breakfast would even *happen* the next day.

I surveyed my surroundings, still in awe with how the outside world operated. There were *so many people*! The noise was incredible as one person after another talked over each other, vendors shouted their negotiations, children ran around playing with each other... I even saw a few stray chickens clucking away in the middle of the cobblestone street.

I looked to Nick, who was still arguing with the grumpy merchant, and slipped away for just a minute, not planning to go too far. I went from booth to booth, admiring all of the various items for sale. There was everything! Things like jewelry, books… I even saw a booth dedicated to selling nothing but corn.

All of a sudden, I felt the leather strap of my satchel slip off my shoulder. I whirled around to see if I dropped it but instead saw a young, dirty boy sprinting away with it.

"Hey!" I shouted. "That's mine!"

I bolted after him, pushing past the angry people in my way, all the while shouting at the child. The boy shot a look back at me, a mischievous grin on his face, and I gritted my teeth in frustration. I tried to move faster, annoyed by my long skirts, and followed him through dark alleyways and tried not to stop at the many rats and rancid smells I encountered.

I caught a glimpse of the boy making a sharp left turn. My breathing was heavy, but I pushed on. Once making it around the corner, I couldn't see the thief anywhere. I screamed and slammed my fist against a wall, barely wincing as it scraped the skin. I needed that bag! It had all of my clothes and money!

I bit back my frustrated tears and looked around. There was just a dead-end in front of me

—an abandoned storefront boarded shut for what seemed to be a long while. With further examination, I concluded the boarding was done too well, and there were no hidden crawl spaces for the thief to have squeezed through.

Finally giving up my search for the child, I decided the best thing to do was to try and find Nick again. But the alleyways I had chased the thief through were like a maze. I had no idea what way would lead back to the market.

Hours passed, and it was beginning to get dark. I curled myself to the slimy ground and leaned against an equally slimy wall, trying not to imagine how they got that way. The possibility of Nick staying in the market to look for me had long passed. He most likely gave up and left me to fend for myself.

I bit my lip to stop it from trembling. There was nothing more I could do in that moment but try to get some rest. There were a few other people around me in tattered clothes and stinking of poor hygiene with the same idea. Many of them stared at me curiously, others with mischievous grins on their faces. I was terrified someone might kill me in the night. I slid my hand onto Father's dagger sheathed at my waist and urged myself to fall asleep.

The next morning proved no better than the day before. Except for the fact that I actually found the market. But it did me no good. Nick was nowhere in sight. Not to mention, my stomach growled painfully. I hadn't eaten for over twenty-four hours, and I had no money to pay for anything.

I roamed through the streets for another full day, accomplishing nothing except to learn that I was in Bothar, the capital of Edristan. In hindsight, the view of the distant towers of the castle should have probably been enough of a hint.

Hopelessness and lack of my productivity in reaching a solution lasted for another two days, and the hunger was beginning to gnaw at me in extremes that I could have never imagined. It got so bad that even the occasional drinks of water I stole from the town well were making it worse. But that wasn't the only discomfort. I looked down at my clothes and saw the holes wearing into the expensive, blue cloak I'd brought with me from home. And the dirt caked on my skin and in my fingernails made me yearn for a hot bath.

I continued with my usual daily wanderings, and without thinking, I found myself back at the alleyway where the boy who stole my satchel disappeared. I recognized it because of the same abandoned storefront at its end. I realized that my subconscious must have held onto the slightest hope that maybe I'd find the boy and reclaim my satchel. The hunger pains and exhaustion were too much of a presence for my mind to remind me that such notions were ridiculous.

I spent maybe five minutes examining the old storefront again before feeling too weak to continue. But before I moved to lie and rest on the hard ground, I heard the faint sound of a chuckle to my left. It seemed to be coming from *inside* the alley wall. I moved closer to inspect it, holding my breath to avoid smelling the mold. The gray stone was very old and crumbled slightly at the touch of my finger. The sound of laughter became even more distinct, and there was no doubt about it: the sound was *definitely* coming from behind that wall.

I ran my hand along the entire wall, remembering the stories of secret passageways in various books I had read in the past. And then I found it! There was a single loose stone, and I pushed my weight against it until it slid past the others, making a clicking sound. I leapt back as half of the wall swung open, revealing a large room with many bookshelves along the walls and a hallway that must have the led to other rooms. Though the space looked poor and was falling apart, it was filled to the brim with a hodge-podge of different items. But that wasn't the most surprising part: in the middle of the room was a long table with seven young boys sitting around it, each of them digging into bowls of gleaming chicken breasts.

My mouth immediately watered at the intoxicating smell.

They all froze and stared at me, jaws hanging open, as I stood in the entryway, watching them eat with longing. And then I recognized him. The little, brown-haired boy that stole my satchel.

"It's you!" I shouted.

Then, without warning, the wall behind me began to slide back into place, and I jumped all the way through before I was caught in it. Placing my hands on my hips, I moved closer to the young boys, not feeling intimidated in the slightest. Even the oldest had to have been two or three years younger than my nineteen years.

"That boy stole my things!" I pointed to the thief.

The boy that had stolen the bag from me flushed as the other boys looked in his direction, but they didn't seem disappointed. It almost seemed like they were *proud*.

"Well?" I raised my voice, the anger I felt making me forget about my hunger.

The boy at the head of the table, blond and incredibly freckled, rose from his seat and began to speak.

"We steal to survive, miss."

That was a simple answer, but it didn't satisfy me. I raised an eyebrow and flipped the dark curls out of my face.

"I still want it back!" I snapped.

The boys looked me up and down, then leapt

from their chairs and huddled together in the corner of the room. I knit my brows together as I saw one little head after another pop up from the huddle to give me a curious glance, then continue with the whispering.

The boys became silent all of a sudden and moved back to their seats.

"Well?" I said.

The freckled boy who spoke to me earlier rose again. "We have decided. You can have all of your stuff back, but..." He paused, grinning at the other boys. "You must earn your keep first."

I chuckled. "You are all just little boys. What's to stop me from searching for my things and leaving?"

Each of the boys pulled out various weapons from their belts, including the two littlest ones who couldn't have been more than five and also seemed to be twins. Considering that I had no idea how to use Father's dagger, and the boys seemed more than familiar with their own weapons, I sighed.

"What do you need me to do?"

The boy smiled with his crooked teeth. "First are introductions! I'm Arnold, and these are my six younger brothers." He pointed to each boy in turn, all of them giving me a little smile or mischievous wink. "Ben, Larry, Jacob, Marv, and the twins are Patrick and Phil."

All seven boys were definitely similar enough to be brothers, especially since they were each unusually short for their ages. But there were also stark differences. Arnold wasn't the only blond, but his hair was more golden than anyone else's. The one called Ben was plump and ruddy, Larry (the one who stole my satchel) was incredibly scrawny, Jacob's blue eyes seemed huge underneath the lenses of his spectacles, Marv was rather fit for his age— he couldn't have been more than ten, and the twins were identical with their orange hair and pale skin.

I folded my arms, wanting to get this over with. "I'm Snow."

"Hi, Snow!" they all said simultaneously. It was kind of creepy.

"That's a weird name," one of the twins whispered.

Then I realized something I hadn't before. "Where are your parents?"

"Oh, them?" Arnold brushed it aside. "They died a while ago. We've been taking care of ourselves for a long time."

I remembered that I was also parentless, but I pushed that thought aside. "Can we get along with this?"

Arnold's smile disappeared, and he cleared his throat. "Fine. Snow, we have rules around here. And one of them is that you have to work to eat." He eyed me up and down. "You seem rather worse for wear, and we're willing to allow you to live here if you do the work we require of you."

My shoulders fell as I was reminded of my hunger and that he was right— I was desperate and needed a place to stay. My attitude changed completely, and I raised my gaze to the lead boy again.

"Fine," I said, defeated. "I'll do whatever you want me to. Just please..." I eyed the chicken on the table and was unable to suppress the urge to lick my lips. "I'm so hungry."

The seven pairs of eyes watching as I snarfed the chicken down didn't bother me one bit. In that moment, it felt like I had never tasted such incredible food in my entire life. The boys were obviously poor, and there wasn't much of it, but I was beyond grateful for even the few bites of juicy meat they were able to give me.

Arnold drummed his fingers on the table, grasping at the knife in his other hand. "Where are you from exactly, Snow?" he said, finally breaking the silence.

I thought for a moment. "Far away."

It wasn't entirely a lie. White Manor was on the south end of Edristan, and I knew that Nick and I traveled for a good few days before even *getting* to Bothar.

The boys stood up and huddled in the corner again, whispering about me. It was getting old.

They then moved back to their seats but didn't put away their weapons.

"We've decided to trust you," Arnold continued. "For now."

I nodded but was so enamored with my meal that I didn't really care if they had decided to trust me or not.

"And that means we'll start your training first thing tomorrow."

Those words got my attention. "Training?"

All the boys grinned, suddenly looking like the brothers they were.

"We're going to make you a thief, Snow," Arnold said.

Chapter 7

"You look gorgeous."

Dalia stood before the massive mahogany door of the throne room, awaiting her cue to enter. She was shaking uncontrollably, and her stomach kept doing flips.

"Dalia?"

Dalia shook her head and glanced at Aeryn. "I'm sorry, what did you say?"

Aeryn knit her brows together in concern. "I said you look beautiful."

The Princess glanced down at herself, not really having noticed what she was dressed in that morning. Her bodice was tied even tighter than usual, and she thought they were too tight in the past. She obviously didn't know how uncomfortable a dress really could be until that moment. Her smooth skirts were embroidered with a beautiful, golden thread that spun into delicate flowers all over the emerald green silk. Her fiery hair was partially braided, but the rest poured over her shoulders in loose curls. However, Dalia was too nervous about caring how pretty she looked.

"Thank you, Aeryn."

Harold, one of the newest recruits to the castle guard, poked his round head through the door.

"They're ready for you, Your Highness."

Dalia took a deep breath and tried to wipe the sweat off her palms.

"You'll do great," Aeryn whispered, then moved to pick up the Princess's long train.

Upon entering the room, the hundreds of nobles and subjects fell silent. The throne room spanned almost a third of their large castle, so it would be a long walk for Dalia down the aisle. The walls were adorned with long tapestries displaying the robust and leafless tree, emblem of Edristan, decorated with the blue and white colors of the kingdom. The sun from outside poured in light through the massive glass windows that extended along every wall. And all eyes were on her.

She gulped. If she could get through the entire coronation ceremony without throwing up or blacking out, it would be a relief.

She climbed the marble steps that led to the two thrones, the deep wood of the seats inlaid with lines of gold and cushioned with red fabric. Her parents' seats. She squinted her eyes shut, trying not to cry, then continued onward.

The priest dressed in his long, white robes was an old man, hunched over to the point that he barely stood taller than Dalia as she knelt in front of him. She darted her eyes about the room, seeing the solemn faces of her people. She knew they were sad for their King and Queen's deaths and were nervous for her to take the throne so unprepared, but somehow that thought gave her the courage to sit up straighter in her position. She was going to be their Queen, and she was determined to take care of Edristan just as well as her parents had.

"Lords and Ladies, Counts and Countesses, people of Edristan," the priest projected to the audience, "we gather for the crowning of our dear Princess Dalia in lieu of King Rory's and Queen Margaret's untimely deaths…"

Dalia humbly bowed her head as she listened to the words. The priest moved to anoint her with the blessing of the religion from ancient times—when all the land was ruled by just one High King. Dalia admitted to herself that she knew nothing of religion, but the priests in hers and many other kingdoms still worshipped the ancient Kings and their ways before civil war broke out, and the Kingdom was divided into five: Greriveth, Mardasia, Polart, Edristan, and Wilaldan. There was peace now, but unity into one kingdom was not likely to happen again.

"With this anointing, I crown you…" He reached down to a table next to him and lifted the large crown, a light blue fabric surrounded by a frame of silver and jewels, and held it above the Princess's head. "Queen Dalia Char of Edristan."

Dalia held her breath as she felt the crown touch her head. The priest then gestured for her to sit on the throne to the audience's right. She gingerly rose from her knees and stepped over, careful not to trip on her skirts. As she sat, the priest led her in the oaths, and she spoke the words of promise to rule with justice, mercy, and compassion. At the end of her words, the priest led the crowd in the Kingdom's customary chant.

"Long live Queen Dalia!" he cried with a voice much stronger than his fragile body let on.

The crowd shouted the words back three times.

There were no cheers, just a respectful silence as they moved from their seats to bow to their Queen. Dalia lifted her chin in acknowledgment to her subjects, refusing to tremble. She survived the ceremony, and she was Queen. The ceremony hadn't been too bad. No one booed her, she didn't get sick... She suddenly felt her heart drop to her stomach as she remembered what her next step was supposed to be: she had to get married.

Chapter 8

"No, Snow! That was terrible!"

I held the coin in my hands that I had grabbed from Ben's back pocket and shot Arnold an annoyed look.

"What did I do wrong?"

"He would have felt *everything* you just did! You practically told him what you were going to do with your body language. Again!"

I sighed.

For the next few weeks, the seven boys were slaving away in preparing me to be a model thief, pickpocketer, liar, you name it. Some things I was good at. I actually handled my father's dagger very well under the five-year-old twins' lessons, when they weren't harassing me relentlessly with their various pranks. And I proved decent at the lying, but for some reason, my stealing wasn't good enough yet.

Rolling my shoulders back, I once again adopted the persona I was using to "steal" from the particular target Ben played.

"Hello, sir," I said while swiveling my hips in the way they taught me. It felt strange.

Aleese Hughes

Ben turned his chubby body to face me, taking on a character of his own. "Ah, hello."

For a thirteen-year-old boy, Ben was very good at acting like a pompous, old Lord. He was the best actor out of the seven boys.

Ben gave me a sweeping bow and kissed my outstretched hand. I had to bend myself closer to the floor to avoid making Ben stand on the tips of his toes. I batted some eyelashes at him, and he giggled, the little boy coming out again.

I yanked my hand away from his grip, exasperated. "This is so weird! Can we go back to where I just pretend to be his friend, then rob him silly?" I turned my attention to the much younger Ben. "It's strange to flirt with him."

Arnold groaned and rubbed his face with his hands. "Let's take a break. Ben, maybe start some lunch with the others. I'm gonna talk to Snow."

I watched as Ben's blond head walked away from me, shaking in disapproval.

"C'mon, Snow. Let's go for a walk."

I followed Arnold through the little corridor on our right, trying to navigate through the mess of dirty socks and rotten food strewn about the place. I had only been living with the boys for a few days, but their lifestyle was not something I thought I could get used to.

Their home was a lot bigger than I initially anticipated. There were four large rooms, one of which they let me use for myself, and not to mention they also had a small kitchen and dining area. When I asked them about how they had found such a place, a place that was hidden, I might add, all of the boys went uncharacteristically quiet and muttered something about their father's strange taste in houses.

"Where are we going?" I asked.

"I'm taking you out for a practice run."

"What?"

He ignored me as we reached the secret door to the outside. He peeked through a small eyehole, not having to crouch down any shorter at all. I would have had to squat a good amount to look through their little hole, being taller than all of them. Every boy was younger than I, even Arnold, but they were still shorter than average. They must have had tiny parents.

"All clear," he said as he pushed in the loose stone to trigger the door.

We both stepped back as it clicked, then swung open.

"Hurry," he hissed at me. "No one can see."

We quickly moved to the warmth of the outside, summer air, and I watched as Arnold closed the door behind us.

"So… what did you mean by a practice run?"

"I'll show you."

Arnold led me back out into the streets I perused with Nick just weeks before. Nick, who was probably long gone by then. The town was just as busy as when I had first seen it. My previous discovery weeks ago that I was in Bothar made even more sense than in my delirious, hungered state. As Arnold and I walked, it seemed so *vast*, and there were just as many nobles around us as there were the lower class people.

Although I was born a noble, I felt like I fit in better with the peasants. Spending your life as a servant to your father can do that to you. But there was one thing I did find myself missing from living at White Manor...

I looked down at my clothes. The brown trousers on my legs drooped past my knees in an un-flattering fashion, and the shirt I wore kept falling off of my narrow shoulders. I missed being able to dress in my pretty things, though it was a step up from my tattered travel dress and cloak, both destroyed from roaming the streets by myself for days.

I did end up finding my satchel Larry had stolen from me, but the comfort of food and lodge while living with the boys was enough to take away any temptation to grab my stuff and run. I was pleased to have my dresses back, however. But, within a few days of wearing my beautiful clothes, the boys had urged that we find me new, more practical clothes for the life I had taken on. They still didn't know of my background, nor I really theirs, but they knew the clothes I had on me were expensive. We sold the few ensembles in my possession, even the travel cloaks, to buy me some loose trousers and a couple of simple tops. Though, I suspected that what they bought me didn't cover nearly as much of the money they had gotten for my garments.

I followed Arnold around the merchants' booths at the market, watching as he shoved small items from the tables into his pockets. He was really good at it.

Arnold pulled me over into a dark corner past the earshot of any vendors or shoppers.

"I want you to try something risky," he said. "The best way to train is to practice in the real world."

He nodded out to the crowd again, all busy with their conversations. I eyed the people myself, beginning to feel anxious.

"Are you sure I'm ready?"

Arnold waved my words away. "Snow, you've been training with us for two weeks now. You're actually pretty good at it."

I gulped. *Training* to be a thief was different than actually doing it. All of a sudden, it felt wrong, and my stomach started doing flips.

"Pick someone random. Anyone. Don't think about it. Talk to them, become their friend, flirt if you have to. Then steal from their bag or pockets without them knowing what happened."

I nodded but still wasn't sure if I was ready to take on the challenge. My nerves started making me feel sick, but then I thought of the hospitality the boys had been showing me for the last while. Soon my nervousness was replaced with determination to be good at what the boys had taught me. I wanted to prove myself.

My eyes found a young woman, most likely of noble blood, walking among the booths showcasing expensive jewelry. She was careful not to stand near anyone of lower rank and turned her nose up in the air at anyone who came closer than a foot. I smiled. Taking a long string out of my pocket, I tied my long hair back out of the way, then moved in the woman's direction.

As I came closer, I began to pretend an interest in a small pair of earrings a vendor was selling at the booth next to where the woman was shopping.

"How much?" I asked the seller.

The pudgy man folded his tattooed arms and looked me up and down in disgust.

"Not for you," he huffed.

I chuckled on the inside. These people knew dirt poor when they saw it. I pretended offense and tried to move away quickly, purposely bumping into my target.

"How dare you— you cretin!" she cried, clutching at her chest. She stank strongly of perfumes and face powder.

"I'm so sorry, m'lady!" I reached my arm out to stabilize her but really slunk my hand down into the large side purse at her hip.

"Don't touch me!"

Her shrill voice made my ears ring, and I watched as she trotted away in a fury. I grinned, fingering the coins I stole from her in one hand,

and the earrings from the vendor who had rudely turned me away in the other. I shoved them in my pockets before anyone could see.

I found myself giggling as I walked back towards Arnold. I was surprised, but stealing gave me a sense of thrill that I grew rather fond of— a feeling that I never felt until I gave my father that pie. The sense of danger and the burst of adrenaline put a grin on my face and made my heart pound at speeds that excited me.

Before I moved to head back to Arnold, I heard two young girls, neither much older than twelve, giggling not two feet away from me. Each had blue, silk ribbons tied into their hair, and they wore bright pink dresses of expensive make. They were most likely daughters of a lord, or count, and their nearly matching clothes helped me deduce that the two were sisters.

The girls were saying something about the Queen and a ball to celebrate her coronation.

Queen Margaret? Wasn't she crowned Queen before I was even born? I thought.

I inched closer to eavesdrop on their conversation, pretending to look at some books on display at the stand next to them.

"Mother told me that Queen Dalia is quite the beauty," the elder, taller one said.

Her sister's eyes widened. "Oh, I wish children were invited to her coronation ball!"

My thoughts were spinning. Queen Dalia? How much had I missed? What happened to King Rory and Queen Margaret? I was always under the impression that our monarchs were good people that ruled fairly and justly. At least, that's what I told myself since I never had much opportunity to learn of the politics and the various happenings within Edristan. But how would Queen Dalia be as a ruler? Wasn't she only eighteen?

I tucked the thought away and continued on my path back to Arnold. But then, directly in front of me, I saw a tall man carrying an open satchel at his side. It was calling to me. Just grab something and get away quickly was all I needed to do.

I moved with the flow of the congested crowd and slid my hand into the bag, making sure the man's face was turned in the opposite direction. I gripped something cold and was about to scamper away when he grabbed my wrist and yanked me around to stand in front of him.

"What do you think you're— Snow?"

I gasped, yanking my arm out of Nick's grip.

"You're— you're still here?" I stammered. The shock at seeing him froze me in place.

"More like *you're* still here! I've been looking everywhere for you! I was worried someone kidnapped you and threw your body into a river, or something!"

It took me a moment to find words, but after processing what he said, I found it hard to appreciate the sentiment.

"I'm fine," I said. "Why do you care, anyway? We hardly know each other." I didn't believe in his concern. If he really had been looking everywhere for me, we were bound to have found one another before the boys took me in.

He set his jaw. "I don't like bad things happening to people. After a couple days of searching, I had to leave to hunt for more food, but I've kept coming back." The look he gave me was intense. "You were just a helpless girl I found in the woods, and I felt responsible for you."

Ignoring his words, I turned on my heel and continued towards Arnold, who still stood in the corner, mouthing the words, "Come on!"

Nick followed me, noticing who I was headed towards.

"Who's that?" he demanded.

"A friend! Really, Nick. I can take care of myself."

He continued to follow me as I continued to shoot back glances at him, eyes narrowed, but he was unfazed by it. He seemed curious and determined to see what I was up to. I found it annoying. We had only known each other for a few days. It wasn't like we were even remotely friends. He *had* helped me when I needed it, but I had barely thought of him since I ran off.

"Snow," Arnold said as I approached, "why is this guy following you?"

Nick stepped up to the much smaller boy and puffed out his chest. "I'm a friend of Snow's. Just wanted to make sure she's okay."

Arnold didn't even flinch, giving Nick a smug look. "Don't worry, she's safe with us. We've been helping her."

Nick barked out a laugh. "What can a little boy like you do to help her?"

Arnold pushed Nick out of his face, wiping the bits of spittle that had been spat on him during Nick's remarks. "My brothers and I have our ways."

Nick folded his arms, trying to process the boy's words. I sighed heavily, getting frustrated by the wasted time.

"Really, boys," I said. "Nick, I am capable of making my own decisions. And Arnold, don't we have somewhere to be?"

I grabbed Arnold's scrawny arm in my hand and pulled him away from the busy market. Nick didn't try to stop me, but I felt his sea-green eyes burning into my back as we sailed away through the crowd.

"I thought you were from 'far away,'" Arnold said, breaking the silence. "How do you know someone in Bothar?"

"I met him on my travels," I said, dropping his arm.

"Are you guys... close?" Was that a hint of jealousy I heard in his voice? Couldn't be... I was three years his senior.

I shrugged. "We barely know each other. I think he just feels a little protective of me."

We walked in silence again, moving further and further away from the most congested parts of town. I found myself scanning the area more than I had before. The stonework of the streets and walls were old. Even the paint on the buildings scattered around us was peeling off. But the place was *huge*. Nothing in my wildest imaginations could have pictured the outside world having so... much. And I hadn't even seen a fraction of it!

I glanced at Arnold. His round face was angled away from me, probably studying the various passersby for possible pickpocketing opportunities. What was it with him and his six brothers? What was their story? Arnold seemed to have taken on a fatherly role, acting much older than his actual age, and the others were able to hold their own pretty well, too.

"Arnold?"

He looked up at me. "Yeah?"

"What happened to you and your brothers?"

His face went dark, and my curiosity peaked. They had obviously been through more than most boys of their ages.

"I don't see why you have to know," he said, keeping his eyes on our path. The sun was already setting, so he sped up his pace, most likely wanting to get home before dark.

I shrugged, matching his strides easily, for my legs were much longer. "I don't. Just *want* to know. You've gotta admit it's pretty weird to find seven orphan boys living in a secret hideaway and stealing to survive."

"Hush!" Arnold darted his eyes about nervously, then wrenched my shoulder nearly out of its socket as he pulled me into a dark corner at his right, far from any people.

"There's a reason we're in hiding," he hissed.

"And what's the reason?"

He rubbed his face with his hands, inner turmoil in his expression. What was so secret that he didn't want to tell me?

"Fine," he finally said. He lowered his voice even more than before. "Have you ever heard of the dwarf race in the Lurid Kingdom? *Very* far west of here."

I found myself laughing. "Dwarves are just a myth."

Arnold's face turned red, and he seemed offended by my words. "Something most people have come to learn about this world, Snow, is that things aren't usually myths."

I thought back to the witch Bavmorda, and the apple that poisoned my father. A lot of things about her had seemed somewhat mythical. If magic was real, why not dwarves?

"Okay," I said. "What does your history have to do with the dwarf race in Lurid?"

Arnold continued to scan the area for any listeners.

"There's no one near us," I snapped.

"If *anyone* hears what I'm about to tell you, my brothers and I will be in serious danger."

The severity in his tone shocked me. I nodded, eager to hear what he had to say next.

"My mother was a noble in the Lurid Kingdom, but she was cast out after falling in love with a dwarf, my father. They ran away together to Edristan and started a family."

I guffawed. "What? How does that even work? He had to have been at *least* two feet shorter than your mother."

He gritted his teeth and clenched his fists. "So?"

I thought of the unusual shortness of the seven boys as I looked down at the top of Arnold's head.

"But that doesn't explain why you're in hiding."

Arnold cleared his throat, wringing his hands together. "People don't take kindly to those who are different. My father was ridiculed by the people of Edristan, not to mention my mother was persecuted for marrying a dwarf. We moved around a lot until Father found the secret home in the alleyway, previously inhabited by thieves. But one day, when picking up some food, Mother and Father were caught up by a mob about three years ago, and—" His voice broke as he tried to hold back tears.

The image of Arnold's parents' deaths by an angry mob turned my stomach upside down. Those poor boys. Then realization struck me like a chord.

"If people learn of yours and your brothers' parentage," I said, "the same might happen to you."

Arnold nodded, shifting his teary eyes away from mine. "People don't like anything or anyone different." He wiped at his eyes and straightened his back. "One day, we're going to get enough money and pay for passage out of here."

"Where would you go?" I asked.

"Where do you think? The dwarves are our best bet for acceptance and..." He paused for a long time. "And for family."

I put my arms down at my sides, twitching as I tried to decide if I should rest a hand on his shoulder in comfort. I wasn't very good at those types of things. And then I had an idea. Maybe I could help Arnold and his brothers.

"Arnold," I said, "what do you know about royal balls?"

Chapter 9

"Larry, pass the potatoes!"

"I'm still getting some, Marv!"

"You already filled half your plate with some! I need to eat, too! Jacob, you're close to him. Flick his ear, will ya, and pass the stupid potatoes?"

I was starting to get used to the noise. Surrounding me on every side were the boys as we sat for dinner late that night. Arnold sat at the head, yelling at one brother after another not to throw food around the room. Ben, the next eldest, shoveled his juicy chicken into his mouth without ever coming up for air. I quickly learned in those few days why he was chubbier than the others. Larry, scrawny in comparison to Ben, especially noticeable as he sat next to him, pulled the glass dish of mashed potatoes to his chest.

"If you want the potatoes so bad, go ahead and take them from me," Larry teased.

Marv leapt from his old, wooden chair, nearly throwing it to the floor, and tackled Larry. Jacob leaned to the right in his own chair, avoiding the fight as he continued reading the thick book in his hands.

"Hey!" the twins Paul and Phil shouted. "You're getting potatoes on our knives!" The twins had brought their impressive collection of sharp knives to the table, cleaning them with great love and care.

I sighed, carefully reaching my hand to the middle of the table to grab a cob of corn. The table wobbled under my arm, precariously standing on its uneven legs. It was a table that had seen many rough days. Scratches and gouges were all along the wood, but that wasn't surprising considering the group of people that ate around it every day.

"Larry, Marv! Sit down, or I will smack you silly!" Arnold said, threateningly pointing a drumstick at his wrestling brothers.

No, the noise didn't bother me so much, but as I looked to the kitchen area and beheld the mess of dishes and food covering the walls and floor, that's what bothered me. I was used to order and cleanliness, having been forced to attain such things all my life, but my roommates probably didn't even know what "clean" meant.

I looked down at my chipped plate, noticing the stains from yesterday's meals still gleaming on its glass. When was the last time they *really* cleaned this place?

I chewed at my own food and remained silent among the chaos, lost in my own thoughts. Seeing Nick again was strange—I didn't think him to care enough to stay in town to look for me. But the idea made me more frustrated than glad. If he really had been looking so hard, he would've found me!

And the seven boys' story hit me hard. The idea that our kingdom's inhabitants would be so cruel and ignorant to people and things that were different infuriated me. Why was there cruelty in the world at all? I found myself clutching at the metal fork in my hand, knuckles turning white from the tight grip.

"Whoa, Snow," Ben said next to me. "You're going to bend our silverware!" Ben placed his chubby, dimpled hand on mine and forced me to set the fork down.

"What's got you so mad, Snow? You always seem so angry," Marv said through a mouthful of potatoes that he finally got from Larry.

I relaxed my clenched fists, trying to process his words. He was right: I *was* angry all the time. But why not? Life was unfair, and no matter how much someone might claim to be, no one was a good person.

"I'm fine," I muttered.

No one questioned me further.

"Boys!" Arnold shouted over the noise. "I have a very important announcement to make."

That's right, I thought to myself, the anger dissipating. I had told Arnold about the upcoming ball in celebration of Queen Dalia's coronation. After a shocking revelation from Arnold that King Rory and Queen Margaret died in a tragic carriage ride accident, thus explaining the crowning of Princess Dalia, I proposed an idea. A crazy idea. But he liked it. And even *I* started feeling excited about it.

The six other boys quieted after a minute or two and looked at their elder brother expectantly.

"First of all, Snow was *brilliant* today." There was a round of enthusiastic applause, and I grinned. I really *did* do well. Arnold held up a hand for more silence. "Anyway, not only was she a model thief, but she proved to be quite the informant and proposed an idea."

All the boys leaned forward in anticipation. I found myself bouncing up and down in my seat, eagerly awaiting their reactions.

"Snow learned of a ball that's supposed to be held in Queen Dalia's honor. After further prodding and questioning around town, we learned it is an open invitation event to adult nobles from *all* over."

I noticed the confused looks on the other boys' faces. They looked disappointed that the ball was the announcement.

"What does that have to do with us?" Jacob asked, pushing his spectacles up his nose in annoyance.

Arnold held up a finger. "I'm getting to that."

Jacob looked as if he was about to protest, but he shut his mouth.

"This ball provides us with an opportunity of a lifetime. Especially with Snow here. We are too young to attend the ball, but Snow is not. And look at her, she can *easily* pass as a noblewoman."

Arnold gestured to me, and I flushed slightly as fourteen eyes studied me curiously.

"She has agreed to infiltrate the ball," he continued with a big, goofy grin on his face. All his brothers began bouncing in their seats, excitement replacing confusion as they realized what Arnold was getting at.

"Hundreds of nobles and loads of royalty will be there partying and dancing," I chimed in. "The perfect opportunity to waltz, flirt, and steal a thing or two."

"Now we just need to teach you how to be a noblewoman," Arnold directed to me.

That might not be as difficult as you think, I thought to myself. Though I lived more as a servant in Father's household, I had been around enough of his noble friends to learn a thing or two.

I left my half-eaten chicken breast, potatoes, and corn on my plate, too wrapped up in the thoughts of the ball to finish my meal. The boys began to slow down with their own eating, and I sat in silence as one by one, they got up and left more of a mess.

"Snow, aren't you gonna go to bed?"

I glanced up at Arnold, eyes narrowed. "Aren't we gonna clean up the mess?"

Arnold yawned and shrugged his bony shoulders. "I don't really feel like it. Maybe tomorrow."

I rolled my eyes as he traipsed away after his little brothers.

I might as well get started, I thought.

There were no windows in the boys' hideaway to show me the darkness of outside, but my weary body was enough to tell me how late it was. It was at *least* past midnight. The boys' schedules for eating and sleeping were so skewed, but who was I to complain? I had nowhere else to go, and I honestly preferred having the same place to rest my head every night rather than trudging through the woods with Nick. I quickly learned that I was not the outdoorsy type as I slept on the hard ground night after night and tried to tune out all the ominous noises that surrounded me in the forest. The hot and sticky summer air was not very helpful, either.

I pinched my nose as I approached the kitchen area. The smell was even stronger in there. I searched the counters in the hope that I would know where to start. After searching through the few wooden cupboards, I miraculously found a relatively clean pot. In the corner of the kitchen, away from the light of the few candles burning, I stumbled around in search of the bucket Marv filled with water from the town's well that morning.

I grunted as I tried to lift the full bucket in my arms, then resorted to bringing the pot over and submerging it in the water to fill it. I picked up the small pot and carefully tiptoed through the mess of the space to move back to the dining area where a fire was still gently burning in their hearth. Their hearth was crudely constructed and much smaller than the one that stretched from wall to wall at White Manor, but it still did the job. Careful not to burn myself, I pulled the handle of the pot over the hook above the fire. I needed to boil the water before cleaning all the dishes, unlike at home. I read somewhere that living in more densely populated areas proved to bring about more risk in having contaminated water— something about fecal matter. White Manor lived in more isolation and therefore had more availability to freshwater.

As I moved to get a broom to start sweeping the dusty, stone floor, I heard some scraping at the hideaway's entrance behind me. I whirled around, heart thumping nearly out of my chest.

Someone found us.

My eyes darted around the room for something, *anything* that I might be able to fight with. Why did I leave my dagger in my room before dinner? Arnold was constantly insinuating how important it is to *always* have a weapon on hand! My eyes flew to the dining table, and I rushed to grab a silver knife by one of the place-settings.

The stones of the secret entrance clicked and began to slide back. Before I could shout for the boys, my jaw dropped open as I saw who it was.

"Nick! How—"

He held up a gloved hand to silence me. "Are the others asleep?" He had his usual pack, bow, and sheath of arrows hanging over his shoulders and the small hatchet at his hip.

I moved to shut the door behind him, then bent to look through the eye hole, searching the night for any onlookers.

"Are you crazy, Nick? If someone finds these boys, they're dead!" I stepped away to put the knife back on the table.

Nick raised an eyebrow. "Is that so? Who exactly are you living with here, Snow?"

I groaned. "I honestly don't see how that concerns you."

Nick began pacing the area, studying the peeling wallpaper on the walls, wrinkling his nose up at the dirty socks and dishes he encountered. I watched as he peeked his head around the corner to the narrow hallway that led to the bedrooms.

"Where on earth did this place come from?"

Before I could answer his question, the water I had put on the fire began to hiss, and I moved to grab the pot before it boiled over.

"It's old," Nick continued. "The stone of the walls is cracking, and the wood paneling along the door frames back there are splintered." He pointed to the boys' bedrooms in the back. Nick had a good eye, considering the rooms were far from where he stood, and the candlelight from the dining area barely even stretched a third of the way down the hallway. "Bothar must've been built around this place."

I ignored him as I wrapped a smelly cloth around the pot's hot handle and scurried into the kitchen.

"Snow," Nick said, following me, "I'm here to help you. I was thinking that maybe you were only living with that boy because you had no other choice."

I snorted. It was true, but I was not about to admit that.

"How did you even find us?"

"I followed you and waited until dark, hoping to sneak you out while the others were sleeping. I really lucked out."

I set the pot down on the floor and leapt back before any of the scalding liquid could hit my bare legs— another negative to wearing knee-length trousers.

"I didn't ask you to come save me," I huffed. "These boys need my help. Once I do what they need me to, they'll help me, and I'll be set for life."

Nick knit his brows together, deepening the sharp angles in his face. "How will you be set for life, exactly?"

I bit my tongue. How would Nick react to the livelihood of the seven boys— how they survive? Would he turn them in— turn me in? Stealing wasn't exactly an admired trade.

"And you keep saying 'they.' How many people are you living with?"

I shook my head and piled up plate after plate in my arms and dumped them in a large basin in the corner.

"If you'll excuse me, I have a lot of dishes to do," I said.

Nick grabbed my shoulder and yanked me around to face him. I rolled my shoulder out of his grip.

"That hurt!"

He ignored me. "Are they thieves, Snow? You tried to steal from me in town today! Are they asking you to steal for them?"

I exhaled heavily through my nose. "If you must know, I'm living with seven orphan boys who want nothing more than to travel away from Edristan in hopes of finding family. There's something I can do to make that possible."

"Seven boys? You're too delicate for something like that!"

I clenched my jaw. "I am *not*! You don't even know me, Nicholas!"

He raised his hands up in surrender. "Sorry, Snow. I just don't like the idea of a young woman getting taken advantage of."

"Snow?"

The sound of a little voice startled the two of us, and I rushed through the dining area to find the source. Nick ducked away out of sight.

"Phil," I said, "What are you doing up?"

"I was going to get a drink of water, but then I heard some voices." The redheaded five-year-old moved his eyes about, scanning the area. "Who were you talking to?"

I jumped as Nick rested his hand on my shoulder.

"I thought you were hiding," I hissed.

"Hey there, little one," Nick said as he bent towards the twin. "I'm a friend of Snow's."

"Careful," I warned.

Nick shrugged me off. "What's a little boy going to do to me?"

Within the next two seconds, before I could even blink, Phil pulled a gleaming, long knife from under his yellow tunic and held it against the scruff on Nick's chin.

"You're an intruder," Phil said, trying to deepen his high voice. "Do you know what we do to intruders?"

Nick gulped. "Uh, Snow?"

"Phil," I said, gently pushing the child back. "It's okay. Nick just thought I was in trouble. He really is a friend."

Phil squinted his eyes at me, suspicious, then to Nick. "We'll let Arnold decide that."

Chapter 10

The ceiling seemed duller than usual. Dalia used to love staring up at the elegant intricacy of the painted sky above her bed. Her mother hired a skilled artist when Dalia was just a child to add some life to the room.

"A child, royal or not, deserves to have an imagination. Let Dalia have the sky."

Those were the words Queen Margaret said all those years ago. Oh, how she missed her mother.

The curve of the dark clouds painted among the twinkling of the stars and the big, yellow moon used to fill her nights with wonder and daydreams of one day getting out into the world and never stopping. Away from the castle, away as a princess, away for an adventure. She had always loved her life— before her parents died, but it didn't stop Dalia's yearning to travel.

But now she wasn't just the Princess, she was the Queen.

Dalia turned to her side as a tear dripped off her thin nose and onto the satin of her pillow. There was no room in her life for daydreams anymore — just a responsibility for her kingdom. Every day was filled with meetings, sitting in the throne room for hours listening to the subjects' needs, and attending event after event to present herself to the noble families as their new Queen. She often found herself looking back on her life as a princess with longing.

A draft from outside blew onto the back of Dalia's neck, making her hairs stand up. Dalia sat up quickly, staring at the large window at the end of her bedchamber.

Had that been open before? she thought.

Another gust of wind blew in from outside, extinguishing the candle's flame on her nightstand. Then the only light in the room came from the glowing embers of the fire that died in the hearth an hour before.

Dalia pushed off her thick covers and gingerly stepped out of bed, bare feet cold against the stone floor. Shivering, she moved to the bay windows and pushed on the panes until they clicked shut.

"Good evening, Your Majesty."

Dalia whirled around to see an old, crooked woman sitting on her mattress. She sat like a young child, with her legs crossed, and was drawing circles into Dalia's quilts with her long, cracked fingernails.

"Guards," Dalia squeaked.

The woman raised a wrinkled hand to her ear. "What was that, child?"

Dalia couldn't find the words as she stood frozen before the intruder.

The woman sighed and reclined back into the many pillows on the bed. "I wanted to give my condolences in person— about your parents' deaths. And my congratulations, too! You'll be a marvelous queen, I'm sure."

Dalia swallowed down the lump in her throat. "Guards!" she cried.

"They can't hear you, dear."

"What did you do?"

The woman waved her question away. "They're just sleeping. They'll wake in the morning."

"Who are you?" Dalia found herself inching further away from the visitor until her back hit the wall.

"Bavmorda. Isn't that a wonderful name? After a lot of experimentation, that's the one I like the most."

"Why are you here?"

Bavmorda sat up again, brushing down her ratted skirts that no amount of fixing could help. "I have a gift for you. A coronation gift, if you will."

Dalia pressed her palms against the wall, trying to push herself as far away from Bavmorda as possible. "A gift?"

Bavmorda pointed to Dalia's vanity. There, leaning against the mirror, was another... mirror.

"Um, thank you?"

Bavmorda clicked her tongue, chuckling. "That is not just *any* mirror. It's special. Let me show you."

With more nimbleness than her body let on,

Bavmorda jumped off the bed and skipped over to her gift.

"Come on," she urged.

Dalia hesitated, but if the woman came to hurt her, she would have already done it. As she approached, Dalia was able to admire the details of the mirror better than in her previous position.

The frame of gold circled the oval shape of the glass and entangled itself in depictions of twisted vines and roses. About a dozen diamonds were encrusted along the frame, as well. Dalia stared at her reflection in the glass. She saw the usual things: the red hair, the green eyes, but this was not a normal reflection. As Dalia leaned forward to decide what exactly was different, her image's pink lips curled up into a gentle smile. She gasped, jumping back.

"What, dear?"

"I smiled!"

"That tends to be a normal thing to do."

"No, it..." Dalia trailed off. She hadn't actually smiled; her reflection did on its own. Dalia shook her head. She had been through a lot recently, and maybe her tired eyes were playing tricks on her.

"Well, anyway, this mirror is magic."

Dalia's mouth dropped open as she looked to the woman who grinned a smile with just a few rotten teeth in her mouth.

"Magic. Are you—"

"A witch? Yes, I'm a witch. Let's move on from that point. It usually takes a long time for people to get over that revelation."

Dalia knew that magic wasn't unheard of in Edristan, but she had never actually come across anything, or any*one*, with those mystical properties. She looked at her reflection again, her image watching her as if it was its own person. The witchery would explain that.

"This mirror," Bavmorda continued as she inched closer to the Queen, "will answer nearly any question and show you any place."

"Nearly?"

Bavmorda nodded, just an inch away from Dalia's face. Dalia held her breath as the witch's rancid smell burned the inside of her nose. When was the last time the woman bathed?

"Nearly because it will only answer questions and show you places that apply to the present, not the future."

"What do you mean?"

"It will show you any person and what they are doing at that very moment. It will also show you different kingdoms and lands when you ask it to."

Dalia raised an eyebrow. "I can spy on people?"

The woman shrugged. "If you want to. I figured you'd like it more for showing you the world. You've always wanted to see what it's like out there, correct?"

Dalia felt her hands begin to shake. It was one thing for this woman to claim to be a witch, but it was something else for Bavmorda to know these things about her. But curiosity got the better of her.

"Show me."

"What do you want to see?"

"Anything."

Bavmorda cackled slightly and cracked her knuckles. "This is one of my favorite questions to ask. It changes every ten years or so. Mirror, mirror on the wall—"

"What are you doing?"

The witch sighed heavily, shoulders hunching over dejectedly. "You have to say those words before your question, or the spell won't work."

"Oh."

"Mirror, mirror on the wall," she continued, "who is the fairest one of all?"

Dalia gasped as the glass of the mirror swirled as if turned to liquid. It spun and spun, flashing a brilliant light towards the two. Dalia squinted her eyes shut, blinded until the spinning slowed to a stop and an image started to fade into focus.

Within the glass was a young woman, maybe a little older than Dalia, resting on a stiff-looking cot. The wool blanket atop her didn't quite come up to her shoulders, so they were still able to see her slender figure. Her long, loose curls twisted along the cot in a divine pile of ebony, and her blood-red lips contrasted beautifully against her fair skin.

"Who is that?" the Queen whispered in awe. "She's beautiful."

"Hmm..." Bavmorda said, rubbing her chin.

"I've met her before. I thought her attractive, but not necessarily the fairest in all the land. The mirror knows better than I, I guess."

Dalia didn't take her eyes away from the mirror and the sleeping maiden.

"You've got to admit, though," the witch continued, "I'm a pretty close second." Bavmorda placed a hand on her bony hip and posed for the Queen, chuckling. "I was sure it would be me in that image."

"Show me more!" Dalia started bouncing up and down on the balls of her feet, feeling excited. "Show me a place! An *amazing* place!"

Bavmorda licked her cracked lips. "You do it, child. It's your mirror."

Dalia rushed to stand in front of the glass as the image of the fair maiden faded away, and her own reflection returned. She searched her mind for the places she'd studied in maps and books, trying to think of the perfect destination.

"Mirror, mirror on the wall, show me the oceans of Wilaldan."

She raised a hand to her mouth gleefully as the glass once again turned to illusory liquid and spun into the image she had asked for.

"Oh," she cried, clutching at her chest. "Look at how blue it is!"

The mirror showed her the crashing of clear, blue waves against the white-sanded shore. It was daytime in Wilaldan, for the sun shone brightly upon the shimmering water and the smooth rocks. Dalia could even hear the crow of what must have been the seagulls she read about in her books. Oh, how she longed to be there and put her bare feet in the water.

"Bavmorda, thank—" Dalia's words were stopped as she turned to thank the witch, but she wasn't there. She disappeared as quickly as she had come.

The Queen turned her attention back to the images of the ocean, fear once again sweeping through her body. Why did the witch think it important to give her this gift? Dalia shivered and noticed the windows were open again.

I guess witches don't use doors, she thought.

Chapter 11

At first, the boys felt more than slight trepidation towards Nick's presence, but soon they all realized the benefits of having a huntsman live with them. Especially the thought of fresh game once or twice a week appealed to their young minds. Even Arnold, who showed the most uneasiness of all, soon came to accept his being there.

But I had a hard time understanding why Nick felt the need to stay and protect me. He did a rotten job of doing so before, so why now? What was his intense interest in seeing me unharmed all of a sudden? It honestly annoyed me, but I had to agree with the boys: having a huntsman around was rather convenient.

The next two weeks was night and day work in turning me into the persona the boys, and I worked so hard to develop. The Lady Isabella: a beautiful and flirtatious force to be reckoned with. She didn't take "no" for an answer, and in turn, she didn't give "no" as an answer, either. She agreed to every dance, strolled through the gardens with every man... And best of all, no one would suspect her of thievery.

"Again!" Arnold demanded.

I rolled my shoulders back and pursed my lips slightly into a pout as I strutted across the room. The boys had moved the dining table into the hallway so I could use the space to practice. They even went as far as to put strewn books on their shelves and clear away some dishes.

"Good," he praised me.

Nick was sitting in a dark corner, sharpening his hatchet with a whetstone. He was pretending to direct all of his attention to the job, but I kept catching his glances at me. I had trouble reading his thoughts through his hooded eyes and dull expression.

"Okay," Arnold said. "Now pretend to flirt with me and take the coin from my pocket." He lifted a shiny copper piece into the light to show me, then placed it in his back pocket.

"She needs someone taller to practice on," one of the twins said. I almost forgot the rest of the boys were watching my training from under the dining table in the hallway. They were sitting in a neat line like ducks in a row.

"Nick can do it!" Jacob said, not looking up from his book.

Arnold frowned, and I could've sworn I could see the jealousy cross his face that time.

"Fine," Arnold said after a long pause.

"Oh, no." Nick shook the whetstone in his hand at Arnold. "I'm not getting involved in your mischievous, dangerous plans." He turned his stark, green eyes to my face. "This is very dangerous, Snow."

I rolled my eyes. "You keep saying that."

Arnold seemed deep in thought. "Actually, Snow, he's right."

My jaw dropped open. "Arnold! Don't start agreeing with Nick all of a sudden! You *need* me to do this job, remember?"

He rubbed his chin, ignoring my words. "I think people would have a hard time believing Lady Isabella would be traveling to Bothar all by herself."

Realization dawned on me, and all eyes turned to Nick.

"What?" he demanded.

"I can't believe I've gotten roped into this."

I leaned on the wood paneling of the open doorway as Arnold, Ben, and Larry made the final adjustments to Nick's loose breeches and the bright green doublet across his long torso. All three stood in front of a tall, cracked mirror in the tiny bedroom I had been occupying the last few days. It took everything in me not to laugh at the sight of Nick in his new outfit. It was the day of the ball, and they were preparing Lord Charmont to escort his beautiful sister, the Lady Isabella, to the event.

"You brought it upon yourself," I said. "Besides, you'll be a lot of help. The boys were right—people would be suspicious of Lady Isabella if she were by herself. Her brother Lord Charmont at her side would make our story more believable."

"That's another thing," Nick said as Arnold instructed him to lift up his right arm. "Why do I have to play your brother? Shouldn't I be a husband or something?"

Arnold scoffed, face turning red. "Why would you need to be a husband... or something?"

Nick shrugged, much to the annoyance of the boys adjusting his ensemble. "I don't know. I just don't look anything like her brother."

"Snow needs to be able to flirt with all the nobles there," Ben chimed in. "It would make some people a little less forthcoming if they knew she was there with a significant other."

"On that note," I said, "shouldn't we be getting me ready, too? The ball is in, what, three hours?"

"Yes, just a second, Snow," Arnold said as he stepped back to study Nick. "Larry, it's too tight around his buttocks."

"My butt?" Nick whirled around to try to look at it in the mirror, and I was unable to stifle my snickering. Nick flushed a deep red, not a thing I expected to see from someone like him.

"Come on," Arnold said to me. "The dress we got for you is in one of the other rooms."

By "got," I was sure he meant "stole." How else were they supposed to get something as fancy as

79

what they put on Nick and what they were un-doubtedly about to put on me?

Arnold led me to the room that he and a couple of the older boys shared down the hall. After a quick knock and no answer, he turned the rusted knob and nodded his head at the gown lying across one the three cots in the room.

"Put that on," he said. "I'll be back in a few minutes."

The older boys' room was much larger than the one they were having me stay in. I was obviously sleeping in a small study of sorts, surrounded by books and a small, rickety desk. The boys' room was nearly empty. Well, except for the clothes all over the floor and their cots.

I moved to the bed in the center and stared at the gown before me. It was beautiful, and I found myself close to tears as I thought about wearing something so lovely again. The bodice was sprin-kled with small, shining stones of silver, and the silk material radiated a flattering, deep red— a color that would compliment my similarly red lips and dark hair.

I happily removed the hideous tunic and trou-sers on my body and slipped into the shift Arnold had set beside the dress. I then followed with the hoop skirt. How were they able to get a hold of these things? Hoop skirts didn't come by easy— even for nobles.

I slipped the dress over my head, welcoming the cool touch of the smooth fabric. There was another tall mirror in this room, and I moved to look at my reflection. I found myself smiling at the image and twirled around to see the gown over my entire figure. It flattered every curve and fit me almost perfectly. The boys really knew what they were doing.

I almost didn't hear the knock as I admired my reflection.

"Snow?" Arnold peeked his head in, hand over his eyes. "Can I come in?"

"Yes."

Arnold put his hand down, then approached me with his head cocked to the side, studying me intently. He stared at me for a moment too long and, after noticing my questioning look, turned his face away bashfully.

"I think that'll do," he said, avoiding my gaze. "We should tighten the bodice, though."

He found the strings at the back of my torso and proceeded to pull and tighten them as far as they could go.

"Whoa," I wheezed, "I might not be able to breathe!"

Arnold swiveled his head around my shoulder and made eye contact with me through the mirror, his past embarrassment having subsided.

"It'll look good, though."

He was right. The tighter bodice flattered my figure even more so than before.

"Now for your hair," Arnold said.

He found a little stool in the far corner of the

room and brought it over for me to sit on. My pile of skirts made sitting on the tiny stool difficult, but after a little adjusting, I was able to do so.

"Marv!" Arnold shouted through the open door and down the hallway. "Can you bring me those hairpins we got yesterday?"

"Sure!" Marv's distant voice shouted back.

"Arnold," I said, "how do you and your brothers know how to do all of this stuff? You found me a great dress, know a lot about the court and their behaviors, and now you're going to do my hair and makeup."

Marv skipped into the room at that moment with a rusted tin in his hands. The pins inside the container clattered as he moved.

I continued: "It's just kind of strange to meet boys who can do what you do, don't you think? Especially orphan boys."

Arnold pulled a white comb from his back pocket and gently brushed the tangles out of my hair that spilled past the top of the stool.

"You know how I said that our mother was a noble?"

I nodded, much to Arnold's chagrin. He grabbed my head and urged me to stay still. Then he carried on with what he was saying:

"Even after becoming an outcast and living in hiding with our father, she never stopped loving nice things. She *always* looked elegant."

He nodded his head at my dress. "That was hers."

"Oh," I stared at the gown on my body again. "I thought you—"

"Stole it?" He chuckled. "We stole Nick's clothes, yes, but what you're wearing is beyond even what *we* are capable of."

"That still doesn't explain how you know anything about hair," I said as he twisted my locks into intricate braids and circled them atop my head.

He shrugged. "I watched Mother in front of her mirror a lot. I pick things up really easily."

"I'll say," I said, staring at the beautiful style he was creating.

"What do you think?" he said after another few minutes.

I twisted my neck back and forth to see the finished product. The pins he used to twist up the loose braids had small, silver stones, a match to the ones on my dress, that sparkled prettily against the black of my locks.

"Wow," I whispered in awe. "My hair has never looked this pretty..."

Arnold folded his arms, proud of himself. "Of course not. Now for the makeup."

I had never actually worn a ton of makeup before— living with my father more as a servant than his noble daughter didn't bring about many occasions that warranted such things.

I watched as Arnold brushed some rouge onto my cheeks and some glittery tan color to the lids of my eyes. I tried not to flinch at the various tools he touched to my face but coughed as he padded some white powder onto my skin.

"What does the makeup do, exactly?" I asked with my eyes shut as he applied something he had called a liner.

"I don't know exactly. Mother always said it makes a woman look her best. You can open your eyes now."

I did and gasped at the image that looked back at me. "That looks… different."

Arnold raised an eyebrow. "You don't like it?"

I shook my head. "No, I look amazing."

"Oh, wait. I got some rouge on your chin."

Arnold leaned forward to wipe away the red smudge. Our faces were close, and I could count the little freckles on the bridge of his nose. His eyes met mine.

"Snow," he whispered.

I leaned back slightly. "Uh, yeah?"

"Do you think after this job, maybe… I mean…"

He stood up straighter, face turning a little red. It made him look younger. Arnold acted and spoke older than his sixteen years, but in that moment, he was a little boy.

"My brothers," he continued, "they need some-one. I need someone. You're— I—" He paused again, shuffling his feet on the floor.

I shifted in my seat, guessing what he might be getting at. I had been suspecting Arnold's little crush on me for days.

"Arnold," I said, "you're very sweet, but—"

"You're older than me." He laughed, nervously running his fingers through his golden hair and moved his gaze to the ground. "What about Nick?"

That surprised me. "What about him?"

"I see the way he looks at you."

I scoffed. "Yeah, right. That would never happen."

Arnold clasped his hands behind his back. "But why not? I mean, he was looking everywhere for you and followed us here, didn't he?"

I pursed my lips into a thin line. I hadn't really thought about the possibility of Nick having feelings for me, but it *was* rather odd that someone I hardly knew was showing so much interest.

Arnold shook his head. "It doesn't matter. Forget I said anything."

"Wow!"

Arnold and I turned to find Nick standing in the doorway dressed up in his fancy noble-men clothes, still looking as silly as before. His breeches were large and puffed out at least five inches away from his actual legs, and the green doublet sparkled in the candlelight.

"You look incredible, Snow!" Nick said.

His jaw was hanging open as his eyes scanned me from head to foot. My face grew hot, thinking about what Arnold said about Nick's attraction to me. I stood up from the stool and avoided eye contact.

"Lord Charmont, Lady Isabella..." Arnold said. "We have work to do."

Chapter 12

The castle wasn't far from the boys' hideaway. It took maybe ten minutes to walk there as we took the back alleyways to avoid any unwanted onlookers—those who might be suspicious of fancily dressed nobles walking around town without a carriage or servants to help them travel to the ball.

"How do we get in?" I asked.

Arnold pulled his black cloak around his face. "Easy. The ball is an open invitation. They're expecting nobles from all over the world. There won't be a list." He looked Nick and me up and down. "And you two look the part well enough."

"What exactly do you need me to do?" Nick chimed in.

Arnold sighed. "Like we said, smile and nod. You are Lady Isabella's brother from the Northern regions— let Snow do the talking *and* the stealing."

Nick narrowed his eyes. "I'm terrible at this sort of thing."

I shot him a glance. "So you've done 'this sort of thing' before?"

Nick laughed. "Of course not! That's how I know I'll be terrible!"

Arnold groaned. "Nick, if you mess this up, I swear—"

"We're here!" I said, interrupting the start to another argument.

Standing so close to the castle was incredible. The structure towered above us to heights where the air was thin, and though the building was old, the gray stone seemed freshly polished. The brilliant light from what had to be *hundreds* of candles shone through dozens of windows. Crowds of people dressed very similarly to Nick and me, some slightly more eccentric, piled in over the drawbridge that stretched over the murky waters of the vast moat.

"Oh my…" I whispered. Everything in me was saying how intimidated and scared I should be, but I found myself grinning, that sense of thrill I had grown so accustomed to bringing about an appealing eagerness.

"This is where I leave you," Arnold said. Without even looking at us, he continued, "Try not to get caught." And with that happy goodbye, he slunk away into the night.

I rolled my shoulders back and adopted Lady Isabella's persona, excited to see where she might take me on this adventure. "Let's go, brother."

One person after another approached the new Queen in an endless line. They kissed her hands, ravishing over her beauty and, as an afterthought, provided sympathies for the loss of her parents.

Dalia felt like her brain had turned to mush as she plastered a happy smile on her face and spoke with kindness to people she didn't even know. She felt lightheaded from the heavy smell of perfumes and powdered wigs as the people passed.

Lord Magnus stood uncomfortably close to her, nudging her shoulder every few minutes or so in reminder to be eloquent, poised, and personable. Her stomach growled as she stole a quick glance at the towering platters of meats and cheeses across the room.

"I usually go to the food first."

Dalia gasped at the words, realizing her yearning stares at the food had been caught. The woman before her laughed melodically, her arm hooked in the tall man's standing next to her. Her golden hair spilled down her shoulders in such a free way, and her blue eyes softened at the horrified look on Dalia's face.

"Don't worry, Your Majesty. I understand the unbearable droll that balls can be better than anyone. Maybe your escort can release you for some food before you're forced to start dancing with boring, old men."

Lord Magnus cleared his throat. "Excuse me, m'lady, and you are?"

"Queen Mildred of Polart, but please call me Milly," the cute woman chirped. "And this is my husband, King Alexander."

The man next to her smiled a crooked smile and adjusted the spectacles on his face. "How do you do?"

Lord Magnus went pale. "I'm sorry, you weren't wearing any..." He was at a loss for words as he gestured towards their bare heads.

"Crowns?" Milly said. "They're so heavy. Especially for traveling."

Dalia touched the enormous crown on her own head. Her sentiments exactly.

The Polart Queen pulled Dalia's hand into hers and gave her another gentle smile.

"Queen Dalia," she whispered, "I'm so sorry for your loss. If there is *anything* Polart can do for you, don't hesitate to call on us." The woman leaned closer. "I'm pretty close to the King and Queen of Mardasia, too." Milly directed her attention to her husband. "Dear, Queen Amelia and King Robert are coming tonight, as well, are they not?"

King Alexander nodded, thoughtful. "That's what the letter said. They didn't leave much later than we did."

Milly turned back to Dalia and squeezed her hands playfully. "You have friends all over the place, Your Majesty. Maybe I'll see you at the food tables later." She gave Lord Magnus a pointed look.

The couple moved away from the line to let others go through. Dalia found that her smile wasn't fake anymore. There was sincerity in Queen Mildred's words, unlike so many of the other guests.

"So odd," Lord Magnus muttered under his breath. "She wasn't even born a noble, you know. Manipulated her way to the throne, if you ask me."

"She seemed nice," Dalia replied, nodding to the other guests as they appeared before her.

"Humph," the Lord replied.

There was a sudden break in the line, and Dalia sighed in relief. "How much longer must I do this for?"

"Not the entire night. Just until Prince Frederik arrives and the dancing begins."

"Does anyone else know of the engagement? The people, for instance?"

He shook his head. "In addition to you and me, just King Alfred, Prince Frederik, and their advisors are the only ones. At least, that was the impression I got."

Before she could say another word, the line started up again. The Queen found herself scanning the faces for her future husband, ignoring the fact that she had no idea what he looked like. Her thoughts wandered to the mirror in her bedroom. She could have asked it... Why didn't she?

Nick was trembling beside me. He didn't strike me as the "trembling" type, but I guess that's what happens when you put a huntsman completely outside his element.

"Why are you so nervous? Just smile and let me do all the work."

"Where do we go?" he said.

"There's a huge line. I thought it was obvious."

I scanned the crowd, feeling the energy of so many people radiating through me. We were still pretty far in the back of the line, not having made it into the ballroom. The hall we inched through was enormous with a ceiling that reached farther than I could almost see. Golden candelabras lined every inch of the walls, providing the space with a festive, bright light.

As I continued to take in the scene around me, I started to make eye contact with one person after another. Once it happened around five times, and the various people began whispering to their companions and pointing at me, I felt like something was amiss.

"Is it just me, or is everyone staring at me?" I whispered to Nick, feeling nervous for the first time.

"Why not?"

I nudged him in the arm slightly. "What is that supposed to mean? I'm serious, Nick."

"Look at you, Snow!" he hissed. "You're the prettiest one here!"

I hushed him, then noticed a lady with a towering powdered wig and a little too much rouge glaring at me from a few feet away. When we made eye contact, she turned her nose up at me and rolled her eyes.

It didn't seem like people were staring at me with suspicion, but was Nick right? Were my looks really that extraordinary to these people?

"You've had to have noticed it yourself," Nick continued. "There's no way you don't know."

Nick was also staring at me, and I began to shuffle my feet uncomfortably.

"Let's just focus on why we're here," I said.

A crippled, old nobleman directly in front of us was continuously pulling a shining, gold pocket watch from his vest.

"This is taking too long!" he croaked. "I *have* to leave not a second past ten! That's in an hour!"

He seemed easy.

"Follow my lead," I whispered to Nick.

I strode up to the man and ran the tips of my fingers along his shoulder. His eyes bulged out of his head as he watched my figure move to stand in front of him.

"It is taking long, isn't it?" I sighed. "My brother, Lord Charmont, and I are bored out of our wits!" I shook my head dramatically, angling my face away and fluttering my eyelashes. "Isn't that right, brother?"

"Yes," Nick squeaked.

I giggled. "My brother is so shy."

The man was grinning at me, which curled his thick, white moustache up to his nose. "Maybe we can help each other to pass the time." He leaned forward and kissed my hand with his wet lips. "May I ask for a name?"

"Lady Isabella." I curtsied. "And—"

"Count Percival," he interrupted.

The line began to move a lot quicker than before.

"Oh!" the Count cried. "Looks like we're finally getting somewhere!" He gave me another eager look. "If you are not otherwise engaged, may I ask for the first dance?"

I smiled. The closeness of a dance was just what I needed to get to that pocket watch.

"Of course."

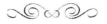

"It is a pleasure to meet you, Queen Dalia."

Dalia watched, speechless, as Prince Frederik bent down to kiss her gloved hand. His thick, dark hair fell halfway over his forehead, and his deep blue eyes never left hers as he bowed. She realized with a shock that she never expected him to be so handsome.

The Prince rose again, towering well over a foot higher than Dalia, and nodded to Lord Magnus in respect.

"This is wonderful!" King Alfred, the Prince's father, bellowed louder than necessary. "You two make a handsome couple!"

Dalia flushed and shrunk even smaller than she was.

The King gently pushed the Prince aside and kissed the Queen's hand in turn. He was much shorter than his son, and his bald head made it hard for Dalia to recognize any similarities between the two. The jovial, plump man turned his attention to Lord Magnus.

"And you must be the Lord Magnus that helped me with creating this arrangement." He enthusiastically grabbed the Lord's hands in his and shook them.

Lord Magnus gave a curt nod, not making any effort to match the Wilaldan King's excitement.

"Why isn't anyone dancing?" The King placed his hands on his hips and surveyed the room. "How drab!"

Lord Magnus cleared his throat. "We were waiting for you. The engagement still needs to be announced."

The King guffawed, shaking his son's shoulder. "Did you hear that, Frederik? They still haven't announced the engagement. I swear, everyone in

Wilaldan knew before my son here did. Attention!" The King moved to the center of the large ballroom, his voice echoing loudly.

Lord Magnus paled. "That's not how this is typically done, Sire."

King Alfred waved the Lord's words away. "Prince Frederik of Wilaldan and your dear Queen Dalia here are engaged to be married! Now let's dance!"

The room fell silent, all jaws hanging open. Dalia caught sight of the announcer at the front of the room. His fists were clenched, and he huffed away, obviously having anticipated his one job for that entire night and angry to have it ripped away so fleetingly.

"Uh…" Prince Frederik chuckled nervously. "May I have this dance, Queen Dalia?" He outstretched his hand, and she took it, avoiding eye contact.

The long line of nobles started to disperse, and the rest of the guests began piling in as the musicians started playing a light tune.

"I'm sorry about my father," Prince Frederik said as he pulled the Queen close to him.

Dalia rested her shaking hand on his shoulder as he placed his on her waist. She tried to force her trembling feet to follow the Prince as he led her to the music.

Everyone was staring at them. The announcement, especially the way it had *been* announced, was probably quite a shock. The people of Edristan didn't just have a new Queen, now they had to come to terms with a prince, of whom they knew nothing about, becoming their King.

"Are you okay, Your Majesty?"

Dalia shook her head and laughed. "I'm so sorry. I'm really nervous."

He laughed along with her. "Trust me, I am, too."

As he smiled at her, Dalia felt her heart flutter. This might not be so bad, after all.

The crowd started to get bored watching the two dance, and many couples joined them on the floor. Others began perusing the food tables and gossiping in corners.

"Who is that?"

Dalia craned her neck to follow the Prince's gaze. Entering among the masses was a tall, slender woman with divinely dark hair twisted around her head. Her red dress hugged her envi- able figure, and the skirts flowed beautifully along with her graceful steps. The Queen knew her from somewhere. Where had that been?

Dalia felt her eyes grow wider as realization struck her. *The girl from the mirror*.

"She's beautiful," he whispered.

Realizing what he said, the Prince shifted his gaze away from the guest and to the floor, a slight blush on his high cheekbones.

Dalia felt a pang of jealousy course through her body, but then she shook it off. She and Prince Frederik had not known each other for more than a few minutes. Dalia didn't expect him to instantly fall in love with her and keep his eyes off of other women. It's not like she felt romantically towards him... At least not yet. Dalia felt her own cheeks grow hot as she thought about her desire for love to blossom between them. That was nothing but wishful thinking. Arranged marriages rarely led to such things.

Dalia glanced back at the woman. She didn't seem much older than Dalia but was definitely taller. The Queen couldn't help but wonder at what the odds were "the fairest in all the land" would show up in Edristan at her ball?

And I thought the ballroom of White Manor was big. I found myself catching my breath as I entered the room, overwhelmed by the dazzling diamonds of the chandeliers, and the exciting noise of hundreds of voices chattering with one another. Shimmering tapestries of blue and white stretched from the high ceiling all the way to the floor, their fabric adorning the strong tree, the symbol of the Edristan Kingdom.

"Isabella, you're blocking the path."

It took me a minute to realize Nick was talking to me. I started at the touch of Nick's hand on my lower back as he moved me out of the entryway.

"It's amazing," I breathed.

I stared, captivated, at the beautiful colors upon the upper-class's clothing and smiled as one couple after another swept into elegant dances in the middle of the floor.

"Is that the Queen?" I pointed to the small body in the middle of all the dancing couples, fiery hair sticking out like a sore thumb. Not to mention the large crown on her head.

"I would assume so," Nick replied.

The tall man she was dancing with gracefully led the Queen in the steps with the music, but I quickly turned away, heart pounding, as I realized the man was staring at me.

"Who's that she's dancing with?"

Nick squinted his eyes a little to see better past the hordes of party-goers. "I don't know."

"That's Prince Frederik, the Queen's betrothed."

Nick and I jumped at the revolting sound of Count Percival's raspy voice. How had he gotten back to me so fast?

"Apparently the engagement was announced just before we came in," the Count continued.

"Where's he from?" Nick asked.

"I heard someone say the Wilaldan Kingdom. Far west of us." The old man quickly changed the subject. "I believe you owe me a dance, Lady Isabella."

The look of eagerness swimming in the Count's gray eyes made my stomach hurt, but I smiled prettily.

"Of course, Count Percival."

Nick gave me a frantic look as the Count, and I sailed past. He mouthed, "What am I supposed to do?"

I ignored Nick's panic and didn't falter as the short man escorted me to the dance floor.

"Let's see if your dancing lives up to those looks of yours."

The Count giggled, and it took everything in me not to crinkle my nose in disgust.

Just as the Count and I got into position, the musicians switched from a light song to a slow ballad.

"Ah, I love this song!" he crooned.

The boys gave me a few lessons in dancing. Which was a good thing, considering my father neglected to provide me with many opportunities for such things in my childhood. But I was apparently good at it because the boys constantly asked, "Are you sure you've never done this before?"

The one thing I was not good at when it came to couples' dancing was allowing the man to lead. It took everything in me not to push the Count in the direction I wanted to go. I took a deep breath and relaxed my body, allowing the clumsy man to direct our steps, even though he was failing miserably.

The golden chain of the man's pocket watch glinted in front of my eyes. I smiled even bigger than before and pushed my body closer to the

Count's. I flinched slightly as I felt his fingers on my waist dig deeper into my skin.

"You dance well, m'lady." He took a deep breath of my perfume then pulled me even closer.

Arnold and his brothers told me that my beauty and femininity was a vital tool to use to my advantage. I tried to remember that as I felt the man's breath tickle the hairs on my neck.

I started drawing circles on his vest with my fingernail, keeping up the flirtatious façade, and slowly slid my fingers around the cold chain. The Count didn't notice as he held his eyes closed, enjoying the music and definitely my company. With one swift movement, I pulled the watch out entirely and pushed it into one of the hidden pockets Larry had sewn into the billowing skirts of my dress.

"Ah."

I jumped as the Count moved away from me, but he just grinned. I blinked, realizing the song had ended.

"It was a pleasure. Truly a pleasure." He bowed, nearly touching his nose to the wooden floor.

"Likewise," I said with a curtsy.

I watched Count Percival giddily skip away, pleased to see he wasn't checking for the time. And by the time he did, he would have danced and socialized with many people— the culprit could be anyone.

I bit my lip to suppress an excited squeal. I was good at this. Like, *really* good at this. And it was the most fun I had in my entire life. I winked at Nick as I glided back to where he was standing and nervously wringing his hands.

"Well?" he asked.

I nodded.

He whistled. "This is insane."

I replied with only a chuckle.

A noblewoman with larger skirts than mine strode past us, giving Nick an alluring gaze and giggling behind her fan. Nick paled slightly and grew stiff. As she moved away, I saw something shiny fall from her ear and bounce against the floor.

Before I could move to inspect it, Nick cried, "My lady, I think you—"

I elbowed him in the ribs before the woman turned to look at us with a questioning, penciled eyebrow raised.

"My brother is shy," I said, trying to think quickly. "But I do think he was trying to ask you for a dance."

She smiled, making bits of her lip stain crack. "I'd love to!"

Nick's jaw fell open, almost grazing the floor.

"Close your mouth," I said, then nudged him towards the plump woman.

As she dragged him onto the dance floor, Nick turned to shoot me a glare. I shrugged, scooping up the dropped jewel. It was a large earring studded with sapphires. A shadow crossed Nick's face as he watched me slide the earring into a hidden pocket. I shook my head, a subtle movement, considering the masses of people in the room, but he understood the message all the same.

I began to stroll by myself along the edges of the ballroom, scanning my whereabouts and absorbing the warmth and energy of the party. Just as I made it to a table piled with a variety of cheeses, I felt the sense that some eyes were boring into me. I whipped my head around in search of the eyes, and there he was. Standing directly in front of me almost all the way across the room was the Prince— the Queen's betrothed. Why did he seem so interested in me?

Realizing I had been staring back for too long, I quickly directed my attention back to the food. But within my peripherals, I could see him begin a slow approach in my direction. Fear gripped at my heart. Did he suspect me? Did he see me stealing the pocket watch or the earring? Was he coming to confront me?

Without any second thought, I briskly stepped behind the table and towards a small hallway. I didn't know where it would lead, but maybe I could lose him. I dared a look behind my shoulder and saw that he sped his own pace to catch up with me. I veered sharply to the left and found an open door. I rushed in but was too slow. The Prince caught up and ran into the room after me.

"Why did you run away from me?" His breathing was ragged, and he moved his dark bangs out of his face.

I gulped. "Uh…"

He chuckled, shaking his head. "I'm sorry. Sometimes I forget that being a prince can intimidate people." He outstretched his hand. "Prince Frederik. And you are?"

I still felt confused as to why he had taken so much interest in me. He cleared his throat, retracting his hand. I shook my head, realizing I hadn't answered his question.

"Lady Isabella."

"I'm really sorry if my following you caused a scare. I just *had* to come talk to you."

I cocked an eyebrow, inching away from him. "Why?"

He shuffled his feet a bit and chuckled as he nervously ran his fingers through his locks. His smile was bright and deepened the dimples on his angular face. He actually was quite handsome. I quickly chastised myself for thinking such things about a prince—a *betrothed* prince.

"This might sound really silly," he said, "but I have never seen someone as beautiful as you. Especially with your *particular* beauty. Your coloring and the black hair is all so…"

I raised an eyebrow, and he laughed at himself again, shifting his gaze to the floor.

"I'm sorry," he continued. "I don't know what's come over me."

I reached the end of the room as I inched away and felt the spine of a book press against my lower back. For the first time, I scanned the room. We were in a small library— a study maybe— but there were still more books piled around us than what we had in White Manor. Continuing to take in my surroundings, I saw that many of the books could be worth a lot of money. There were even a variety of small items and décor that I could easily get away with… if I wasn't in the room with a prince.

"I was hoping I could ask you for a dance."

It took me a moment to process his words, making him feel even more uncomfortable for being so forward. He twiddled his thumbs awkwardly, avoiding my eyes. Suddenly my nervousness left me, and I felt giddy as I realized what was actually happening. How many chances would I get in my life to dance with a *prince*? Besides, that's what Lady Isabella would do.

I took a deep breath and smiled, once again adopting the flirtatiousness and confidence that one Lady Isabella possessed.

"Why not?"

Chapter 13

He was so handsome. That thought kept running through my head as the Prince's steady hand rested on my waist. Why was that the only thing I could think about? I wasn't nervous about being in the presence of a prince anymore— I was amazed and even a little excited about it. Prince Frederik's eyes bore into mine intensely, and I found it challenging to keep his gaze.

All the other couples stopped dancing to watch. Actually, the entire *crowd* was watching us. I could hear the whisperings as we gracefully glided across the floor. He was an incredible dancer and was easy to follow. I could understand why people were staring: in addition to the fact that the Prince of Wilaldan was before them, the two of us must have looked very striking as a couple, and I found I enjoyed the attention.

"You dance extremely well," I said, finally mustering up the courage to start a conversation.

The Prince's eyes still hadn't left my face, and he smiled. It was so charming I felt a shudder through my entire body.

"And you as well, my lady. Tell me, where are

you from?"

I paused, almost having forgotten where Lady Isabella was meant to be from. The Prince's closeness was intoxicating and quite distracting. He noticed my hesitation and cocked his head.

"Lady Isabella?"

I subtly shook my own head from my stupor. "Yes. I'm from the north. Of Edristan."

He nodded and continued beaming that perfect smile, once again revealing a dimple on each cheek. My own smile grew.

The sweet ballad we were moving to ended, and I began to pull away. But before I could move even an inch, Prince Frederik's grip on me tightened, and he squeezed my hand.

"One more dance?" he said playfully.

I opened my mouth to protest, all of a sudden feeling uncomfortable by the curious eyes as the Prince and I didn't part, but no words came out. He swept me to the beat of the next song, a quicker, lighter tune, and I didn't fight it.

We talked for that entire song, laughing and giggling together. I had forgotten entirely about Nick wandering aimlessly by himself, and my purpose there... Until I saw her. The new Queen Dalia was standing in a corner near the musicians. Her red hair that must have taken hours to fix up for the party was starting to fall out from all the dancing she must have done, but she still looked radiant. Her mouth was dropped open to the floor as she watched me in the arms of the Prince. Once she and I made eye contact, it seemed to startle the Queen. She moved her hand up to her pink lips and sprinted out of the ballroom and out of sight.

Then I remembered... I wasn't there to make friends— *especially* not to make friends and flirt with a prince engaged to the Edristan Queen!

Before the song reached its end, I slid myself out of the Prince's grip and gave a quick curtsy. He stood frozen, confused by the abruptness of my movement.

"Thank you for the dance, Your Highness." And then I strode away in search of another victim to steal from.

Dalia sank to the floor in her bedchamber, a feeling of emptiness overwhelming her body. Not only did the loud party, the unwanted attention, and the sense of inadequacy as Queen shake her to her core, but the sight of her newly betrothed dancing in the arms of The Fairest, a new nickname Dalia coined, affected her. Why did he seem so enthralled by The Fairest? The look of admiration on his face as he twirled the tall girl to the music stabbed Dalia with jealousy and even a little anger. The sight made her feel sick, so she had retired early.

Dalia found herself desiring the same look from Prince Frederik that he had given The Fairest. She had hoped they would have a "love at first sight" moment, as people call it. Or that he would at least be taken by her beauty and personality. Something!

"Ugh!" Dalia cried as she threw her face into her hands. Why couldn't anything ever go right?

Dalia wiped her hot tears away and lifted herself from the floor, a feat from the heavy, blue skirts of her dress weighing her down. She moved to the mirror the witch gave her the night before and stood directly in front of it. Though Dalia was frowning deeply, her eerie reflection smiled back at her.

"Mirror, mirror on the wall," Dalia whispered, "show me the fairest one of all."

The glass swirled and flashed as it faded into the image of The Fairest. She was still at the ball. It obviously didn't matter if the new Queen, the guest of honor, wasn't there with these people. All that mattered to the nobles attending was the chance for a party. The Fairest was giggling with yet another man who seemed to absolutely adore her. The young woman wasn't pushing away any of his advances. In fact, she encouraged it with her eye batting and hip twirling.

Dalia rolled her eyes. She knew a lot of noble-women like that— craving the attention and admiration of one suitor after another. If that was the type of woman Prince Frederik was into, maybe Dalia wanted nothing to do with him. But did she have a choice?

The image in the mirror interrupted the Queen's thoughts as The Fairest slid her hand over the belt of the nobleman she spoke to. Dalia watched in horror as her white hand pulled the coin purse tied to his waist with ease and slipped it into the folds of her skirts, all without missing a beat in their conversation.

Dalia gasped, wondering if she should call on the royal guards. But many people would wonder how the Queen knew of The Fairest's crime after having retired for the evening. The image in the mirror faded away, and Dalia's abnormal reflection returned and merely shrugged back at her.

The Queen threw herself onto her bed and stared at the mural on her ceiling. There was nothing she could really do, but maybe she would never even have to see that girl again— the same went for Prince Frederik. Dalia found herself eased by that thought and, still dressed in her ballgown, her exhausted body was able to fall asleep.

Chapter 14

"How'd you do?"

"What'd you get?"

"Was it amazing?"

The numerous shouts of the surrounding boys put a grin on my face. I had gone out, done a job, and I was ready to deliver. I pulled all the knick-knacks and bits of money out of my pockets and poured them out onto the dining table where the seven boys, Nick, and I sat. I folded my arms and sat back, pleased with myself, and eagerly awaited the excited chatter.

"That's it?" Arnold asked. He and his brothers were picking at the items in displeasure.

"That's more than you've ever brought home in a day out in the market!" I snapped back.

Arnold shrugged as he poured the gold pieces from a coin purse I stole. "That's true, but we were expecting..."

"More!" the twins finished for him.

I sat back and tugged at the bodice of my dress uncomfortably. I was starting to notice how tight it was again.

"That's gotta be enough for a month's worth of

food!" Nick defended me. "You should have seen her. No one suspected her, and she pick-pocketed one person after another. I say 'job well done.'"

The boys ignored him, but I knew what they were thinking: they needed more than enough for a month's worth of food. They continued to study my earnings. My eyes started to feel heavy, and, despite my disappointment, I felt the need to rest my head.

"I know you boys don't think I did, but I actually worked really hard tonight." I pursed my lips and glared at each of them. "So I'm off to bed."

Before I gave a chance for anyone to answer, I pushed my chair back, brushed my dress down, and trudged away to my bedroom.

Laying down proved to be difficult with my gown, but I found I did not care. All my thoughts consisted of were frustration— no, anger that my earnings were a failure in the eyes of the seven boys.

I'd like to see them do better, I hissed up at the ceiling.

After another few minutes of fuming to myself, I was surprised as my thoughts slowly shifted to the Prince. Thinking of the way he looked at me, and the strength he demonstrated as he swept me through our dance made my face grow hot. He really was very handsome. I bit my tongue and chastised myself for acting like every other star-struck woman out there. And it wasn't like I'd ever see him again.

The next day I was rather determined to not be around to bear the disappointed looks of the boys and Nick's ridiculous words of defense for me. I decided to go out to the market and steal until I could bring home more than they could possibly imagine. And I was going to do it as the Lady Isabella.

I looked down at the ballgown I was still dressed in and furrowed my brow. I couldn't exactly wear it in the market. Besides, it's silky fabric had been wrinkled in my sleep. And if anyone who was at the ball was in town, I didn't want them thinking I'd wear the same dress two days in a row. *Not* something a lady would do.

"Where would the boys keep their mother's dresses?" I muttered to myself.

It was still early morning, so everybody was still asleep. I took the opportunity to search in every corner within the hideout. And then, out of sheer luck, I found a plethora of luxurious dresses and gowns in the closet in my own bedroom. Figures.

I perused the outfits, searching for a practical one for a visit to the market, yet still eye-catching. Lady Isabella would never look anything less than fabulous. And then I found it. A dark blue, linen dress that fell straight, but I could tell it would hug flatteringly against my curves. The boys' mother had definitely been a very similar size to me.

It took a great deal of effort to untie the red ball-gown and pull it off by myself, so I was grateful for the ease of putting on the blue dress. The linen felt nice against my skin, and I once again smiled at my stunning reflection. It was a simple ensemble, but the cut and cloth were obviously expensive. I pulled out the pins in my hair from last night and fingered through my locks until they fell elegantly past my waist. I definitely looked the part.

I was careful to stay quiet as I tip-toed through the hideout and to the secret entrance. Nick slept in the corner to my left on top of the same bedroll he used while camping outside. I flinched as the wall slid loudly after I pushed the stone to activate the mechanism, but Nick merely stirred and continued with his sleep.

I sighed in relief and slipped out. Though Bothar's alleys and streets had once been an impossible labyrinth for me to navigate, I finally was able to traverse the area and easily find the market. The sights and sounds excited me like they usually did as I slowly walked among the booths with my back straight and head raised. The vendors were more forthcoming to me than when I had looked poor. To them, in that moment, I looked to be a noblewoman with a lot of money to spend.

I stole one knick-knack or coin one after the other and threw them into a small side purse I had also found in the closet. I was having a splendid time. No one suspected me, and I was *so* good at lying to and stealing from the half-witted and daft nobles.

And then I saw him. Penetrating through me were those incredibly blue eyes from across the square, watching me just as he had done at the ball.

I froze in place, but my heart wouldn't stop fluttering. What was Prince Frederik doing in the market? I admitted to myself that I enjoyed the attention as his eyes didn't leave my face. He seemed shocked, yet pleased, to see me, but he made no move to say hello. He was with a small entourage of soldiers— not Edistranian. They were dressed in a bright yellow and white, Wilaldan's colors. A few men must have traveled with him to Bothar.

Realizing I still stood frozen in place, I shook my head at my thoughts. I took the Prince's appearance as a cue to leave. With another two or three glances I threw his way, I realized his eyes still bore into me, and I decided stealing might be hard to keep secret with someone watching me so intently.

I half expected the Prince to follow me as I left, considering how interested he seemed in my being there, but he didn't. After making it out of sight, I studied the new items and money in the

Apples and Princesses

purse. It was a good day, but I knew I could do even better.

As I got home, the boys were very pleased with my initiative and encouraged me to take Lady Isabella out for a run the next day. I was thrilled at the prospect and ignored Nick's grumbles.

Another day in the market, but this time I wore a sweet lavender dress. It didn't flatter me as much as the blue had, but its golden beading and elegant hemline made up for it. Lady Isabella still had no issue grabbing things from various people and booths, but I was once again stopped as Prince Frederik soon appeared in the same spot as the day before, but this time he had no soldiers with him. He watched me, and I couldn't help but notice the small smile on his lips. My heart fluttered at the sight of him, but instead of freezing in place, I smiled back at him.

One day after another proved to be the same, and I quickly realized the Prince was coming to the market at the same time as me on purpose. And I noticed that I started going with the desire to see him on the forefront on my mind rather than going out to earn my keep. And against everything that told me not to, one day I decided to approach the Prince.

"Good morning, Sire," I said with a curtsy.

His white teeth gleamed as his smile grew. "Lady Isabella." He bowed in return. "It's a pleasure seeing you here today."

I suppressed a giggle. We both knew the two of

115

us visiting the market at the same time was no accident.

"If I may, Lady Isabella," he continued. "No lady should be strolling through the market by herself. May I escort you?"

Without waiting for my reply, he tucked my arm into his and led me around the booths. My eyes kept flitting back to my arm in his. Our closeness, just like when we danced at the ball, was intoxicating.

The Prince and I fell into this routine every day for another week, but instead of staying in the market, we began walking together in less congested areas. I tried to avoid thinking about the reason for this— he probably didn't want to get caught spending so much time with another woman while he was betrothed to the Queen. But in places where there were fewer people, Prince Frederik was less likely to be recognized.

"Lady Isabella," he said to me one morning. "There is a beautiful, quaint garden in town. It's in northside, I believe." He avoided my eyes, nervous to continue. "Would you like to meet me there? Noon tomorrow?"

My breath caught. A part of me felt happy that he wanted to set up a rendezvous, but the other part realized the garden in northside was rarely busy, and it was just another place for him to spend time with me without being seen. He noticed my hesitation and frowned.

"I'm sorry. Was that too forward?"

I squeezed his arm. "Oh, no. I'll be there."

Chapter 15

The boys were starting to notice a change in my behavior. Especially as I brought fewer trinkets home every day.

"Snow," Arnold said as I placed a single necklace and just two or three coins on the table. "What's going on with you?"

I felt myself blush but cleared my throat. "What do you mean?"

Everybody gave knowing, concerned looks to one another, including Nick.

"You're humming around the house every day, and you're starting to lack in the earnings you bring home," Ben chimed in through a mouthful of porridge. "The humming *especially* is not like you."

I raised an eyebrow. Humming? Was I?

The long pause and the constant stares the boys gave me made me realize I still hadn't said anything. I didn't want to tell them I was spending my days dawdling with a prince. And then a thought struck me. I was going about it all wrong! All this time, I had been flirting with Prince Frederik instead of taking advantage of the situation. He was most likely wealthy, and if I could milk the relationship we were developing, I might be able to get a thing or two out of him. I palmed myself in the forehead. Why didn't I think of it before?

Because you like him, my inner voice said. I pushed it away.

"I did stumble across an interesting opportunity."

All eyes were on me again, and I felt giddy once more. "There is a particular someone who has taken quite an interest in me."

Arnold raised an eyebrow. "Oh?"

"Who *doesn't* take a particular interest in you, Snow?" Nick grumbled. And then realization dawned on him, and he shook his head at me violently. "He danced with you *once*, Snow! And he's betrothed! There's no way you'll ever see him again."

"Who? Who?" some of the younger ones persisted.

"A prince," Nick said before I could.

The boys' faces lit up.

"Is that so?" Arnold said, unconsciously licking his lips greedily. "What prince?"

"Prince Frederik of Wilaldan. He wants to meet with me tomorrow afternoon for a stroll of some kind—in the city."

Nick turned red beside me and clenched his fists. "Wait, you saw him?"

Anthony waved Nick's words away. "What does that matter? If Snow can woo and manipulate a *prince*, imagine what type of things she can get out of him!"

I nodded eagerly, trying to suppress a giggle. "That's what I thought."

Nick groaned. "This is a very bad idea."

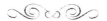

It was a little past noon, and I sat on a bench overlooking a small garden in the northside of Bothar, just where Prince Frederik asked me to meet him. It was hot and muggy, and I found myself wishing the boys had picked out a dress a little more lightweight than the long-sleeved, poofy monstrosity they made me wear.

"It is *very* important you look your best for the Prince," each one of them had said to me. Even the little twins. Their livelihood was riding on this. If I could do well with the plan, they might be able to make it to Lurid after all.

And how did I feel about the situation? I had to stop myself from bouncing up and down due to the excitement oozing out of me. It almost felt like a challenge I was more than willing to prove myself by. My thoughts kept turning to the various imaginations of what I could manipulate out of the Prince.

"Lady Isabella?"

I straightened my spine and turned to the deep

voice.

"Prince Frederik," I spoke smoothly. "I wasn't sure you would actually show up."

He chuckled but darted his eyes around nervously. "Why not?"

I raised an eyebrow and followed his eyes around the area. He was probably still nervous about getting caught with me. But there weren't many people around, not to mention people who would actually recognize who he was.

"Because you're a prince!" I teased. "A *betrothed* one at that."

Prince Frederik flushed deeply. "Shall we stroll, my lady?"

He outstretched his arm to me, and I took it. Though the garden was small, it was well-tended and equally as beautiful as the one at White Manor. I had often found refuge among the rose bushes and green shrubbery at home. And at the moment in Bothar, I admired the gorgeous green around me as we walked the small cobbled path spinning around patches of daisies and rows of tulips.

"I don't want to be engaged, you know."

The words shocked me.

"At least not to someone I don't know," he continued. "Queen Dalia seems wonderful. I just hate that one day I was living my life, and the next I was told to drop everything and get married to a stranger."

"Why are you telling me this?" But I knew why.

Prince Frederik clenched his jaw. "I have no idea." He knew why, too.

"I think I understand how you feel, though," I lied. "My family is from the Northern regions of Edristan, as you know, and they sent me here with my brother as escort to find me a husband—a rich husband."

I eyed the Prince with a sideways glance, reading his reaction. He just seemed thoughtful.

"We are very broke," I finished. My body trembled slightly from the exhilarating lie. The theatrics were enjoyable to me.

"And you don't want to marry just for money." He sighed. "We're both in a tough spot, aren't we?" He studied me quizzically. "Why didn't you tell me any of this before?"

I froze, scrambling for a good excuse. "I didn't want you to worry about me." I breathed out in relief as he nodded at my answer.

He led me to another bench under the shade of a tree, far away from onlookers. I sat down close to him and leaned forward, tipping my head to the side ever so slightly. I knew I needed to prod him a little bit more. If he was as interested in me as I suspected, just a little further manipulation might do the trick.

"Why did you ask me here today?" I whispered. I could see the hairs on his neck stand up as my breath made contact.

He seemed to relax and smiled. I pushed away the inner voice that told me how charming his smile was. The time for enjoyment of mine and the Prince's meetings was over. I had a new purpose.

"I have really been enjoying our time together," he replied, just as I decided to ignore my own enjoyment.

I thought back to our dancing when we met and our conversations days afterward. It *had* been pleasurable... Those moments when the thoughts of future beguilements and deceit were not the forefront of my mind— moments where I only thought of how funny and sweet the Prince was.

I blinked, snapping myself out of my reverie, and turned my attention back to the task at hand.

"I did, too." Not a lie, but still a good thing to say for what I needed to happen.

His smile grew bigger. "I apologize if this is forward, but I feel very drawn to you, Lady Isabella."

I felt my face grow hot and cleared my throat. "Thank you, Your Highness."

He inched forward, and I found myself leaning towards him even more than earlier.

"I've never seen someone with your beauty."

I tried to hide my red cheeks with my hands. His words and closeness made it impossible for me to think straight. The gray specks in his blue eyes swirled prettily as he stared into mine, and his dark brows relaxed as he placed a hand on my knee. My breath caught in my throat, and I mentally pinched myself to remember why I was there. And he was vulnerable.

I rested my own hand on his and forced a tear to spill out the corner of my eye and roll down my cheek.

"Oh, Sire—"

"Frederik," he interrupted.

I smiled. "Frederik, if only things were different! We are both doomed to marry for duty. If only there were some way to change that."

Frederik sat back, thoughtful. "There might be something I can do... At least for you." He pulled the small, leather bag tied at his waist and handed it to me. "Will this help your family for now? Until I can think of something else to help you?"

I eyed the bag, forcing myself not to look smug. "Sire, I can't."

"Frederik. And please, I want to help." He forced my hand open and placed the bag in my palm. I could feel the coins inside shift in my grip.

"Thank you," I whispered.

Frederik looked over his shoulder, searching for any eavesdroppers before continuing. "Will you meet me again? Somewhere more private next time?"

I searched his nervous face, feeling pleased with my abilities to draw him in deeper than he already had been. "Where?"

"Outside the capital. At those ruins."

I pursed my lips into a thin line. "That's a half day's travel by horse."

He nodded. "I know. Tonight I am dining with Queen Dalia, but tomorrow I have no other engagements. I'll just tell people I'm in need of a ride and some alone time."

I raised an eyebrow. "Will people buy that?"

"You'd be surprised how much you can get away with as Prince. As long as I'm back the next day, it should be fine."

I began racking my brain as to how I'd get a hold of a horse. But it wasn't like the boys, and I didn't have money. I thought about my spoils from the ball, and the money the Prince just gave me.

"What time?" I asked him.

"An hour before sunset. I'll be waiting." The tall man stood quickly and bowed to me. "Until tomorrow."

I watched as he briskly stepped away and told my heart to stop fluttering. This was just business, nothing else.

Chapter 16

A panicked knock sounded on Dalia's door.

"Will you go see who that is?" she asked the maid who was brushing her hair.

"Yes, Your Majesty." The chubby girl curtsied and hobbled over to the door, pulling it open just a crack.

Aeryn burst through the door, pushing the poor maid aside and huffed over to the Queen.

"I *have* to tell you what I saw!" she exclaimed.

Dalia eyed her lady-in-waiting questioningly.

"You can leave us," Aeryn directed to the maid. "I'll finish preparing Her Majesty for bed."

The maid looked at Dalia, but the Queen nodded. "It's okay, Maisy."

Maisy curtsied once again and shuffled out of the bedchamber, closing the door behind her with a soft click.

"Well?" Dalia pressed.

Aeryn began pacing the room, fuming. "That good for nothing, piece of—"

"Aeryn! What is it?"

The young woman skidded to a stop and pressed her fingers against her temples. "I saw him

—your Prince."

"So?"

Aeryn shook her head. "You don't understand. I saw him strolling in a garden with *another* woman."

Dalia knit her brows together. "When?"

"This afternoon."

The Queen cleared her throat, trying to ignore her first assumptions. "Maybe he was trying to be social and kind to my people."

Aeryn shook her head vehemently. "It was the same woman he danced with at the ball!"

Dalia felt as if a rock dropped into her stomach as she started to fear the worst. "He danced with a few... What did she look like?"

"That *gorgeous* one with the black hair and impossibly fair skin!"

A groan escaped out of the Queen's lips, and she placed her face into her hands. "Why didn't you say anything at dinner?" she said through her fingers.

"I wasn't about to out his infidelity in front of so many people! I wanted to see what you thought first."

Aeryn, with little to no grace, plopped onto Dalia's mattress with a heavy sigh— the Queen and her lady-in-waiting had more of a comfortable friendship than a master-servant relationship. Dalia watched her friend, debating with herself about whether or not she could trust Aeryn with the knowledge of her magical mirror.

Dalia sighed. "Come here. I need to show you something."

Aeryn bolted upright from her position and moved over to where the Queen sat.

"Hey, why do you have two mirrors? And one on top of the other, might I add."

Aeryn moved to inspect the intricacies of the frame surrounding the magical glass and whistled. "It's beautiful, though."

"It's magic."

Aeryn cocked an eyebrow, pausing for an uncomfortable second or two, then burst into laughter. "Where did *you* get a magic mirror?"

"It was a gift," Dalia huffed, refusing to explain more.

"Fine." Aeryn shrugged. "What does it do?"

"It will show me anything, anywhere, and any-*one* I ask it to. As long as it's in the present."

Dalia's lady-in-waiting narrowed her stormy eyes and studied the Queen's face.

"You don't believe me."

Aeryn smirked. "If it's true, why don't you show me?"

"Fine!" the Queen snapped back as she brushed her hair out of her face. "Mirror, mirror on the wall —"

"It's not on the wall."

Dalia shot Aeryn an annoyed glance, and the lady-in-waiting raised her hands up in surrender.

"Mirror, mirror on the wall, show me the fairest one of all."

Aeryn gasped and took a step back as the lights from the mirror flashed before her eyes until the glass presented the image of The Fairest.

"That's her!" Aeryn exclaimed. "What— How —"

"I don't know. It just does it."

"And she's the fairest one of all? What does that mean— she's the prettiest in all the land?"

Dalia nodded, trying to subside that all too familiar feeling of jealousy.

"What's she doing?" Aeryn whispered as she leaned closer to the glass.

Dalia squinted her eyes to study the scene. The Fairest was surrounded by seven little boys and a young man as she counted a small pile of money on a dingy-looking table. Their surroundings were dirty, old, and falling apart— not a place a noblewoman would be spending a lot of time in.

"That's an odd place for a lady to be," Aeryn said, voicing the Queen's thoughts. "And what's with all the boys and the money?"

Dalia's eyes grew wide. "Are they her accomplices?"

"What?"

Dalia shook her head. "She's a thief! I watched her steal from someone at the ball! These must be the people she works with."

"Little boys and a random young man?"

"She must not really be noble," Dalia continued, ignoring Aeryn's comment.

A spark of realization ignited in Aeryn's eyes,

as well. "Do you think she's using the Prince for money?"

Dalia tapped her fingers on the wood of her vanity. "Maybe…"

"Well, we have to stop her, right?"

The same helplessness that Dalia felt the other night when she watched The Fairest steal through the mirror overwhelmed her.

"We have no proof."

Aeryn snorted. "Proof? You're the Queen!"

Dalia grimaced. "I don't want to use my power to arrest someone I can't prove guilty."

"Show the mirror to the guards!"

It was Dalia's turn to laugh. "And let people know I'm spying with a magic mirror? We have to find another way."

Aeryn began pacing the room again, sure to wear a hole in the floor. "We could have the Prince followed next time he leaves the castle."

"By whom?"

A grin stretched across the girl's face. "By me."

Chapter 17

I squirmed, trying to find a comfortable position in the saddle atop the horse the boys and I bought. We came to the conclusion that buying a horse to travel to the Ruins of Keross and get more out of the Prince was a good investment. Her name was Clover. She was old and a little worse for wear, but she would do the job just fine.

"Here's your satchel," Jacob said as he handed the leather strap to me.

"Thanks." I tied its strap where a saddlebag would typically go.

Jacob shrugged. "I packed it with some food and water for the journey."

I looked over to Arnold, who had also accompanied Jacob, Nick, and me just outside of Bothar to see me off. He gave a curt nod. That gesture meant he trusted me to follow through with the plan. And I would. I was enjoying the adventure and the lies that came with deceiving a prince. At least, that's all I *told* myself it was. I was not about to admit the butterflies and heart skips I felt when thinking about seeing Frederik again.

"Something bad is going to happen to you,

Snow." Nick stood under the tall horse I straddled. He squinted his eyes up at me, a grimace on his face. "This is dangerous."

I clenched my fists around the reins in my gloved hands. "Why don't you just leave, Nick? If you disagree with everything *so much*, just leave."

He clenched his jaw and held my gaze for a second more before dropping his eyes to his feet.

"I care about you, Snow," he whispered.

My stomach clenched as I stared at him. Arnold had been right. Nick had feelings for me— feelings I had no intention of reciprocating.

"That doesn't mean you can make decisions for me!" I snapped. Clover whinnied nervously underneath me as I raised my voice.

"Why do you think so many men stare at you? Or even *fall* for you? Not just strangers, not just me, but a prince! It's not right for you to toy with people like that!"

I threw my head back and laughed. "That's what makes it so perfect!"

Nick rubbed his eyes with his hand. "Then you're not as kind as I thought you were."

My laughing did not stop. "Kind? You thought me *kind*? You have *no* idea what I have done, or what I am capable of."

"But you're helping the boys—"

"You think it's for them? I *enjoy* this! I was *born* to lie and manipulate."

"Uh…" Arnold interjected. "I hope that doesn't mean you'll deceive *us*, Snow."

I shot the short boy a glance and smirked. "You and your brothers would be nothing without me, Arnold. Let me do this job, I'll help you get out of Edristan, and then we'll go our separate ways."

All three stared at me with their jaws open. I shook my head, ignoring the guilt I felt at their surprised faces. Something inside me had snapped. I was tired of all their coddling.

"I must be off," I said, then clicked my heels deep into the horse's flank and rode away.

Hot tears bit at my cheeks as the wind forced them out of my eyes. Why was it that people always felt the need to control me? First my father, then Nick, and even the seven boys? I focused my eyes on the dirt path before me. I would show them. I would show them the power I had over people, and my abilities to do a job well. And who cared what Nick thought about using my beauty to take advantage of a prince? If anything, this is what I was born to do— this is *why* I had my looks. To ridicule and belittle arrogant men— like a prince, who I'm sure deserved whatever was coming to him.

I blinked twice, shocked by an inner voice telling me I was wrong about Frederik— that he wasn't like my father, or anyone else... that he cared about me. My hands began to shake, and my breathing became quick.

"Whoa, Clover," I said while pulling on the reins. "I think I might be sick."

I leapt from the saddle and ran to some bushes

on the side of the road. Though I felt terribly nauseous, nothing came up, but my body wouldn't stop shaking. I could feel drops of sweat trickle down my face, and I bit my lip to keep from screaming. What was wrong with me? I thought of Frederik and his kindness towards me, and Nick's words ran through my head over and over again: "It's not right to toy with people…"

I took deep breaths to try and calm my anxiety. Why was I starting to feel so guilty? Where was the thrill I usually got from the lies and stealing?

"I was wondering when I might see you again."

I whirled around to find an old woman on the path I left Clover on. Something about her seemed so familiar, but it took me a moment to remember. And then it hit me: she was the witch from all those nights ago. The woman I stole the apple from, but this time she was pulling a handcart with what seemed to be a large pumpkin. A *very* large pumpkin that definitely warranted the need for the handcart. What was her name again? Bav…?

"Bavmorda," the witch said, seemingly reading my thoughts. "And you're Snow, of course."

I darted my eyes around us, making sure no one was around us to hear the use of my real name, especially someone like the Prince.

"You look terrible."

I swallowed and exhaled slowly, trying to bring the color back to my face. "I'm fine."

Bavmorda snorted loudly. "Of course. Why

wouldn't you be?"

I narrowed my eyes at the sarcasm. "What are you doing here? And with a pumpkin? You always seem to have produce with you."

A shrill cackle erupted from the woman's cracked lips. "This is for someone who needs it," she said, reaching behind herself to pat the orange skin of the pumpkin. "Doesn't concern you. And don't try to steal it like you did my apple!"

I folded my arms, no longer surprised by her comments. "You dropped it."

"And you killed your father. I wonder which one of us is in the wrong?"

My lips twitched slightly into a smile, and a shadow passed across the witch's dark eyes as she noticed.

"You're definitely an interesting one." Bavmorda shifted her grip on the handles of her cart and began pulling again. "You should know that certain prices are demanded to be paid when such magic is used... Especially in the way you used that apple. Well, I'd better get going. This pumpkin won't get itself there."

I shook my head. "I don't know what that even means, but I have to go, too."

"Just don't fall in love!" she yelled to me as she passed.

I felt my heart stop, the thought of Frederik presenting itself for a moment. "What?"

Without turning back, the witch replied, "It probably won't work out for you. See ya soon!

Bavmorda took a sharp left turn on the road. I watched as her disfigured form hobbled away, feeling confused and frustrated. I shook my head. She didn't know what she was talking about. I wasn't meeting the Prince because I loved him, but because I needed his money. Right?

"Ugh!" I shouted to no one. Clover started at my shout. "It's okay," I whispered to the horse as I mounted her once again.

Frederik said he'd meet me there, so he was maybe an hour or two ahead of me, and I, myself, still had a few hours to go. I inhaled deeply and turned Clover to the right, the opposite way the witch was headed, and I was determined not to let anyone else tell me what I could or could not do.

The Ruins of Keross were just what the title suggested: ruins. Ruins of the citadel of Keross centuries ago when the five kingdoms of Wilaldan, Edristan, Polart, Mardasia, and Greriveth were all ruled by one High King. The land was once called Ennalon. The Kingdom of Lurid, far west, was a landmass just as big as what the five kingdoms occupied. Though what once was Ennalon became five distinct, separate kingdoms, Lurid was still ruled by their High King Rian. The story went that civil war erupted in Ennalon, thus creating the five, separate kingdoms. The Lurid Kingdom must have done, and was still doing, something better than we were.

I took in my surroundings, still in awe of what Keross once was. The chipped stone of the cobbled streets and the dried-up fountains stretched for miles. It had to have been much bigger than Bothar, for sure. I could almost imagine the festive colors of subjects going about their daily routines in such a grand city as Keross.

Directly in front of me loomed a dark tower, teetering dangerously to the side. It must have belonged to the famed castle of the High Kings. What was the last Ennalon High King's name? I racked my brain, flipping through my memories of dusty old history books I read when hiding from my father. High King Bryce! That was it. It was rumored he was taken with a mysterious madness while his people not only turned against him but each other. What marvelous, strange things would be awaiting me inside those crumbling walls?

I'd always wanted to travel to Keross, and just standing outside the ancient gates piqued my sense of adventure and excitement. I wanted nothing more than to explore.

"Lady Isabella!"

I started as the Prince called my name from inside the ruins, almost having forgotten why I came. He sat upon a precarious-looking ledge overlooking some land to our left. I swung my legs over Clover as he rushed over to help me from the saddle.

"You look beautiful," he said.

I flushed. Prince Frederik had this inexplicable power over me every once in a while. A power that made my mind stop all of its normal function. And then I looked down at the silver cloak draping over the light blue dress I wore and inwardly agreed with his sentiment.

"Thank you," I said, straightening my spine and regaining some composure.

After my feet touched the ground, he swept my hand into his and pressed his lips against it. I tried to push away the heat that once again started rising into my cheeks.

"I thought we might watch the sunset together. You're just in time."

He led me over to where he had been sitting and offered his hand to help me to my seat. My breath caught at the sight before us. And then I knew why he chose this spot, dangerous as it seemed. The view was incredible. As the sun began to set, its rays bounced off the swirling clouds in elegant hues of oranges and purples.

"The sun looks so big," I whispered. The view at White Manor had never been such as this, blocked by the tall trees of father's expansive forest. And not to mention I didn't often get a chance to watch the sunset at home, having been expected to serve Lord White's evening meals.

"That's because it *is* big." Frederik chuckled.

"Well, I mean... Just look at that."

The field below us stretched far and flat, providing an illusionary perspective on the expansive horizon. It was almost as if I could touch it.

"I know what you mean," Frederik said. He inched his hand over to mine and rested a single finger on top of my wrist. It was subtle, but I could tell he desired the closeness to me.

I felt my heart flutter again and forgot to be annoyed by the feeling as I shifted my pinky to rest on his hand. Out of the corner of my eye, I watched as Frederik's lips twitched into a smile.

"I was thinking," he said, "about how I could help you." He enthusiastically turned his face to mine with a sparkle in his eye. The look he gave me of pure admiration and desire was intense, and I found my thoughts starting to muddle together again.

I gulped. "Oh?" This was my chance. If he was to offer money, or even jewels, I should take it and run. No sense in prolonging this façade any longer.

"I am the Prince of Wilaldan, heir to the throne. And do you know what I realized?"

The jovial tone to his voice actually put a smile on my face. "What?"

"That I don't have to marry Queen Dalia if I don't want to."

My brows furrowed, and I moved my hand away from his. "I'm sure that won't go over well."

He shook his head. "Oh, it won't. But I have a plan."

I held my breath, fearing what his next words might be.

"We'll run away," he said. "And once things blow over, I'll return home with you. I am the only rightful heir to Wilaldan, and if we're…" He paused for a long time and stared nervously at his feet.

"If we're what?"

He rolled his shoulders back, still not looking at me. "If we're already married, they can't turn us away."

I leapt up from my position and glared at Frederik, eyes wide. "Married?"

Frederik adopted a newfound confidence and stood up next to me, grabbing my hands. I squinted my eyes shut as I tried to process what he was saying to me.

"You can't tell me you haven't felt it, too."

I dared to look at him, biting my lip. "Felt what?"

He squeezed my hands even tighter. It almost hurt. "Our connection. From the moment I set eyes on you… when we danced… every time we're together. I think I love you, Isabella."

Before I could even blink, Frederik pulled me close to his chest and pressed his lips against mine. He smelled of leather and grass, most likely from the ride, but it was invigorating. I found myself moving my hands over his arms and felt the pulsing of his muscles as he drew me even closer to him. I felt my own body relax as I curled into his touch. He pulled away and gazed into my eyes.

"And once we're in Wilaldan, I promise to help your family."

"My family?" I said, still swaying from our embrace.

He raised an eyebrow quizzically. "They sent you to marry wealthy and help their financial situation?"

My stomach did flips, and I felt myself tense up once again. I'd actually forgotten why I was there.

"Of course," I croaked out. The ease and thrill I normally felt from lying had fled from me, and I felt helpless.

A rustling in some bushes from behind startled the both of us. I watched nervously as Frederik let go of his grip on me and pulled a sword from his hip.

"Stay behind me," he hissed through gritted teeth.

I fingered my own dagger, Father's dagger, hidden in a pocket within my skirts. I was confident in my abilities to help if the need arose, but showcasing my skills with a knife might set off alarms to my false identity. I would only use it if I had to.

"Who's there?" Frederik barked in the direction of the movement.

A young woman poked her blonde head above the shrubbery, cheeks a deep red from the embarrassment of getting caught.

"Don't hurt me," she said as she rose, arms lifted in surrender.

"Aeryn?" Frederik exclaimed, jumping back in shock.

"You know her?"

Frederik turned to me, a look of horror etched in his features. "She's the lady-in-waiting to the Queen."

I clutched at my chest as a gasp escaped my lips. Aeryn's fear seemed to dissipate in that moment, and she placed clenched fists on her hips. She leaned her willowy figure towards us and clicked her tongue disapprovingly.

"Boy, do you two have some explaining to do."

Chapter 18

Frederik sheathed his sword, but my hand stayed gripped around the leather hilt of Father's dagger.

"How did you find us, Aeryn." Frederik approached the woman slowly, worry lines etched into his forehead.

Aeryn nodded her head to a horse tied half a mile down the road. "I followed you." She folded her arms. "What are you doing? You're betrothed to the Queen."

He nodded, glancing at me over his shoulder. "I know. But I love Lady Isabella. Do you really want to stop that?"

My stomach started churning again. I was there to manipulate wealth out of Prince Frederik, not destroy the marriage alliance of two kingdoms. But something in me found delight in Frederik saying he loved me, even though my own feelings were too confusing.

"I doubt she loves you back!" the woman exclaimed. She turned her nose up at me and scoffed.

I gritted my teeth. What did she know?

"She's a thief!" Aeryn continued, beginning to

advance towards me. "The Queen and I saw. She's just using you, Your Highness."

My knuckles turned white as I gripped my weapon even tighter.

"How dare you talk to me, or the Lady Isabella in such a manner!" the Prince spat. "You will apologize."

Aeryn narrowed her eyes at me. "I will not. I demand her confession."

Frederik turned to me, a pained look swimming in the blue of his eyes. "What is she talking about, Isabella? Tell her she's wrong."

I gulped, the anxious feeling that overcame me earlier starting to present itself again. The hand around my dagger began to sweat, and my sudden weakness made the grip hard to maintain.

"Isabella?" he pressed.

Before thinking it through, I whipped out the dagger from my skirts and held it towards the two of them. I took a deep breath, refusing to let my emotions weaken my stance. The hand holding my weapon stayed surprisingly still.

Frederik's fingers twitched at the hilt of his sheathed sword, but he hesitated in drawing it.

"What's going on?" His voice trembled as if he didn't want to hear my answer.

"I need money," I said. "Or jewelry. Anything!"

"But, I told you I can help—"

"Now!"

Aeryn and Frederik glanced at each other nervously, and he finally found the courage to draw his sword against me.

"Isabella," he said, "you don't have to do this."

"My name is Snow!" I shouted. "And I only flirted with you to steal from you." I realized those words weren't entirely true, but there was no longer any chance for me to be with him.

The Prince's face fell, and he lowered his sword. I took advantage of the moment and leapt towards the lady-in-waiting, roughly pushing her in front of me and pricking her long neck with the dagger's blade.

"If you don't do what I say *right now*, I swear I'll slit her throat."

"I don't want to hurt you," he said, lifting his sword up again.

"I'll do it!" I screamed through the tears streaming down my face. When had those started?

I pushed the blade deeper into Aeryn's flesh, and little droplets of blood spilled down her front.

"Your Highness," she whimpered, "do what she says. Please."

Frederik frantically searched his pockets. "Oh, wait!" he cried, remembering. "My bag. It's with my horse over there. I packed a good amount of money for our... For our journey together."

He pointed to the clearing and his horse tied to a tree— close to where he'd kissed me. I shook my head, refusing to think about that moment.

"Get it," I snapped.

My head began to throb ever so slightly from the uneasiness of the situation, but I barely noticed it as my heart ached. I watched Frederik sprint to his strong-looking palfrey, a common steed among nobles. The horse's muscles tensed under his dark coat, sensing his master's discomfort. Frederik's confident posture had started to shrink, almost portraying how dejected he was feeling. I squeezed my eyes shut for a moment.

Stop it, Snow, I chastised myself. *You're getting what you came for.*

"Here."

I threw my eyes open to find Frederik before me, holding out a satchel about the same size as mine.

"Take it all," he said.

I slid my free hand from behind Aeryn's back and outstretched it towards the Prince. "Hand it to me. Slowly."

Aeryn was still shaking beneath my grip, making it hard for me to hold the heavy bag as Frederik placed the strap in my palm. I started inching backward towards my own horse.

"I'm going to leave," I whispered, trying to stop my own voice from shaking. "I'll let her go, but don't follow me."

The Prince stood firmly in place, but his lustrous blue eyes penetrated into my own. His gaze was hard, but my lip trembled slightly as a single tear streaked down his cheek.

I held Aeryn's arm as I moved to mount Clover, but let her go just as soon as I began to climb. The young woman fell to the floor and quickly scurried away on her hands and knees, sobbing. Frederik rushed over to console her, but never took his eyes off of my face.

"How could you do something like this?" His voice sounded stronger than earlier, almost angry. "I trusted you."

Despite all the turmoil inside of me, I lifted my chin. "It's what I do."

I eyed the Prince and the sword at his hip, but he made no move to stop me. He seemed to have noticed where I stared, and he shook his head.

"Just go. I meant what I said: I don't want to hurt you."

Before my annoying inner voice could tell me to throw myself into the arms of the handsome Prince and beg for forgiveness, I started Clover at a steady sprint. And I left. Far away from Frederik, far away from Bothar, and far away from everybody.

I didn't know where I was going, but I knew there was no way I could go back to the seven boys and Nick. There was no way to know if Prince Frederik or Aeryn, or both, had alerted the royal guard of my crimes. I couldn't risk it. I didn't know if Frederik would want to publicize his affair with me while engaged to Queen Dalia, but I had no doubt Aeryn would talk. She also said the Queen knew of my thievery... But how? At the ball? Did they see me with the Prince before and suspect my integrity? I shook my head. It didn't matter anymore.

After riding briskly for two hours, only slowing once in consideration of Clover, I pulled over to the side of the road next to a small brook. It was about time my horse had a longer break. I tied her reins to a nearby tree and watched distractedly as she lapped up the clear water from the bubbling water. I finally decided that I might as well look at what the Prince had in his pack.

I untied his satchel from Clover's saddle and avoided smelling the leather material that smelled so much like Frederik. I ripped open the flap and studied its contents. There was a variety of dried fruits and meats tucked away, but in the middle was a large, cloth sack. I pulled the material open and marveled at the pile of gold coins littered with a few silver, and a copper or two. I whistled.

"This will last me a good while," I said to Clover. She whinnied in response, then continued to quench her thirst.

He was serious about running away with me, I thought.

An overwhelming feeling of guilt bubbled inside of me, but I pushed it away. I did what I had to do. This was surviving. But then the guilt rose up inside me once more as I thought about Arnold and his brothers— even Nick. I was abandoning them, but there was no other choice! I was the one in the most immediate need. I needed to get away from Bothar and start anew. The boys had gotten by without me before, and Nick would inevitably get over me.

I calmed my breathing, convinced by my reasoning. Yes, this was the right choice. I looked at the money before me again. With it, I could stay night after night at some inns. Though, I'd never actually stayed in one before, but I assumed the mound of money would be more than sufficient. But where was I to go?

Clover seemed finished with her drink, and I sighed. There was no point in planning a route now— especially when I knew little to nothing of the land and where things were. For the moment, the best thing to do was to trudge onward.

Chapter 19

Queen Dalia watched The Fairest in the mirror. Though the young woman was riding far away from Bothar, Dalia couldn't help but still worry.

"Dalia," Aeryn whispered over her shoulder, "she's leaving. There's nothing to worry about anymore."

Dalia looked to her friend and studied the small cut on her neck, paling. Aeryn touched the wound and chuckled half-heartedly.

"It wasn't so bad," she said. "And you know how long I've yearned for adventure."

Dalia sighed heavily. "She could've killed you!"

She shrugged. "But she didn't. And she really seemed like she wanted to leave."

The Queen twirled a red curl in her finger and directed her attention back to The Fairest as she rode through the night on that sickly-looking horse.

"I hope she doesn't come back."

Aeryn shook her head. "Even if she does, the guards and soldiers know to look out for her from now on."

The image in the mirror faded away, making the

room dark once again, save the one lit candle by Dalia's bed.

A knock, hesitant and soft, interrupted the Queen's thoughts. She moved to answer the door, but Aeryn held up a hand in response.

"I'm still your servant," she said. "Allow me."

Dalia stared at her laughing reflection while Aeryn went to answer the door.

"Oh, look who decided to show up."

Dalia whipped her head around to see to whom Aeryn was referring. Prince Frederik stood in the doorframe, looking abashedly at his feet, cheeks a brilliant red.

"Aeryn!" she scolded.

"It's alright," the Prince assured her, lifting his eyes from the floor. His cheeks turned an even deeper red at the sight of Queen Dalia in her nightgown.

It was Dalia's turn to blush. "I'm sorry," she said. "Give me a minute or two, and I'll be more presentable."

Aeryn slammed the door in his face before he could reply, and Dalia clicked her tongue.

"Aeryn, he's still a prince."

She huffed. "Yeah, an *unfaithful* prince."

Dalia gestured for Aeryn to find a simple gown as she spoke: "We barely knew each other, and he really cared for that woman. It's not like we were in love with one another."

Aeryn raised an eyebrow and pulled a casual blue dress from the Queen's wardrobe in the corner of the room.

"I can't believe you're defending him! I know you like him— even if just a little."

Dalia cleared her throat uncomfortably. "Hush, will you."

The lady-in-waiting slipped the Queen's nightgown off and slid the modest gown over her head.

"It's your life," Aeryn said as she moved back to let the Prince in. "And you're the Queen."

Prince Frederik's eyes were still squeezed shut. "Can I look?"

"Why would I open the door for you again if you couldn't?"

"Aeryn, really," Dalia snapped.

Aeryn rolled her eyes and retreated to the washroom connected to the Queen's bedchambers. The Prince chuckled nervously as she left the room.

"I understand why she might be angry. She's really loyal to you."

Dalia's arms were stiff at her sides as she studied her betrothed, searching for something off in his features. She almost expected him to start spewing off a bunch of lies.

"I'm sorry," he said instead. "I'm so sorry. It was very wrong of me to have done what I did, and I beg your forgiveness."

She felt taken aback by the words and was left speechless. He ran his fingers through his dark hair, awaiting a reply.

"Why?" she squeaked.

It was his turn to feel shocked, and he even

stumbled slightly.

"There's no real answer," he said after a lot of thought. "But I thought I found something with... her I never thought I'd be able to experience."

Dalia inhaled sharply at his words. "Love?"

He nodded, meeting the Queen's eyes.

"I understand that," Dalia sighed.

The Prince shifted from foot to foot, and Dalia could almost see the wheels turning in his mind as he tried to form his next words.

"I still believe a marriage alliance between Wilaldan and Edristan to be beneficial. I know I made a mistake, but I plan on remaining faithful from here on out." He clenched his jaw, still making eye contact with the Queen. "If you'll still have me."

Dalia heard a soft groan from the washroom behind them. She should have known Aeryn would try to eavesdrop.

"I'm willing to put things in the past," Dalia said. "But I won't be so forgiving a second time."

Chapter 20

The shining red of the apple in my hands. The knife as I cut it into slices. The pie I watch Father take bite after bite of. His trembling body followed by empty eyes. The seven boys taking me in. The seven boys laughing at the table, throwing food at each other. Arnold telling them to stop. Nick rolling his eyes beside me and whispering to leave with him. Frederik's fingers in my hair as we kiss. Frederik's face as he learns of my deception. Frederik's broken heart as I ride away. The witch—she cackles in my face, so close I can smell the rank of her breath and count the dozens of wrinkles crinkling in her skin.

"Don't fall in love," she says. "It won't work out for you."

I woke up with a scream, throwing myself upright in the bed I was in. My hair was nearly drenched from sweat.

"Miss?"

A soft knock sounded on the door as a tiny serving maid pushed it open a crack.

"Miss, are you alright?" She held out the stub of a candle towards my face to study me.

I shook under the white linens on top of me, trying to remember where I was.

"Miss, you shouted awf'lly loud just now." Her bumpkin accent was heavy, not from a city, or anywhere near Edristan, for that matter.

"Did I?" I said, rubbing my face.

I took in my surroundings, memory starting to return. I stopped for the night in the first inn I could find, not caring what the expense might be. It seemed I had picked a nicer one. The room was spotless and even had its own washroom, small though it was.

"You did," the girl continued. Her brown eyes were wide with worry, making her look even younger than she was. What was she? Fourteen? Fifteen?

I shook my head and tried to laugh it off. "It was just a nightmare. I'm sorry if I disturbed anyone."

"Oh, no miss." The girl smiled warmly. "It's nearly noon. I was actually coming to check on you. The innkeeper said you only paid for the night and was expecting you to leave after breakfast like most people do."

I looked outside the window behind me, noticing the light streaming through the curtains for the first time. I groaned.

"Was I really asleep that long?"

The girl nodded.

"Well," I said, "tell the innkeeper I'm willing to pay more if he needs me to. I think it will take me a bit to get going."

"Of course, miss."

Before she could leave the room, I stopped her. "Are you still serving food?"

The maid smiled at me again, eyes crinkling up into thin lines. "We've just started serving lunch and will be for the next two hours."

My stomach rumbled. All I had eaten in the last twenty-four hours was dried-up meat and fruit. I needed something substantial.

"Wonderful," I said. "I'll be down soon."

The young girl nodded her head quickly and scurried out, shutting the door behind her. I threw myself back onto the mattress. It was definitely much more comfortable than the cot the seven boys had me sleep on for the last couple of weeks.

The boys.

I groaned, feeling the guilt crawl up inside me once again. And that nightmare didn't help one bit. What did it even mean? That my subconscious was disappointed in my choices? And why had that witch become such a recurring person in my life?

I looked over at my reflection in the vanity across from me. My long hair was disheveled, and my eyes looked sunken in and dark. Regardless of the sleep I had supposedly gotten, the tiredness I felt had not subsided.

I ran my finger over the wood of the table before me and stared at the steaming bowl of soup. Though I knew I was starving, I couldn't find a desire to start eating.

"Bread is really good with chef's broccoli soup." The same serving maid from earlier placed a hunk of fluffy bread on a plate next to me.

Noticing I didn't even move my eyes to look up at her, she continued: "You look pale, miss. I think some food will do ya some good."

"What was your name again?"

The girl straightened her spine, seemingly thrilled to share this piece of information with me. "Hanna— after my late grandmother. She was quite the lady."

A small smile came from my lips. "Beautiful name."

"What's your name, miss?"

I hesitated, not sure as to who might be looking for me and if I should share my name with Hanna, but a shout from across the room decimated any plans I had of concealing it.

"Snow!" a familiar voice called.

My eyes flitted in front of me to find Edgar, a loyal footman to my father, waving me down. He had a shocked look on his face, and his hazel eyes kept studying me up and down.

"That's such a unique name!" Hanna exclaimed.

I blinked twice and tried to give the girl another smile. "If you'll excuse me…"

I lifted the soup and bread in my hands, careful not to spill the hot liquid of the soup on my hands, and carefully hobbled over to Edgar. He leapt from his chair, scraping and bumping loudly, and took the food from my arms and placed it down for me. I nodded in thanks and took a seat across from his place-setting.

"We've been looking everywhere for you!" The older man moved to sit again and reached his arm out to touch my shoulder. "Are you alright? What are you doing here?"

"I've had… an experience," I replied in hushed tones, not able to answer his questions.

He studied me again as worry lines continued to crease his wrinkled forehead. "We thought something happened to you after your father was killed." His eyes grew wide in realization. "Oh, did you know about your father?"

I didn't have much time to think through his words, but they gave me enough to assume the servants of White Manor didn't know the culprit was me. I let my jaw drop open.

"W—what?" I stammered. I was once again pleased with my acting abilities.

Edgar moved his hand over my own. "We found him alone in his study. No one knows what happened, but a doctor suspected poisoning."

I lidded my eyes and shifted my gaze to the floor.

"Oh, Snow," he said. "I'm sorry. We thought whoever got him had you."

"I could see why someone *might* want to poison him." I bit my tongue, not having meant to speak those words aloud, but Edgar didn't seem fazed in the slightest.

"He was not a good father, was he?"

I shook my head, a real tear escaping out of the corner of my eye.

"What happened to you, Snow?"

I looked up at his face and saw the confusion swimming among the gold specks in his eyes and quickly tried to think of a believable story.

"I ran away. I couldn't take the abuse anymore. I thought— I thought I could manage on my own somehow." That much was true, but a hint of thrill pierced through me as I concealed my crime from Edgar. It felt really good for that intoxicating feeling to return.

He merely nodded, rubbing his chin. "No one could blame you for that." He leaned forward and lowered his voice. "If you want to come home, you will be mistress of White Manor, Snow."

Astonishment struck me in that moment like a stab through the heart. He was right. I hadn't thought of that even for one second before. He regarded me with affection, like a grandfather would his granddaughter, and awaited my response. I thought of how wonderful it would be to own and run the Manor... to have a comfortable consistency of luxury, food, and even money. Father had not been poor. But then my thoughts turned back to the fact that I was a fugitive. Would camping out at White Manor, just a few days south of Bothar, be riskier for me? But then again, no one had pursued me thus far.

"Edgar," I finally said, "take me home."

He sat back, an incredulous look crossing his face.

"What luck?" he exclaimed. "I was traveling to visit my daughter and my new grandbaby last week. What are the chances that on my way back, I'd find you, Snow?"

I found myself smiling. Maybe it was fate.

Chapter 21

I was settling into things nicely at my old home. It turned out I had a knack for running things — leading the servants in their cleaning schedules, keeping Father's textile business afloat... The White family was one of the most highly respected for the material they provided for merchants and traders alike, even having some of the textiles making it to port in Wilaldan and traveling to Lurid. The Queen herself wore dresses made from our fabrics. Multiple rooms in the Manor were dedicated for producing and packaging these materials, and at least half of the staff were hired just for that purpose. I, myself, worked in those rooms many times during Father's life. The business in this export had been in my family for generations, providing a steady flow of income, and I was going to keep it that way.

The haunting memories of White Manor that I had been afraid to face didn't plague me nearly as much as I'd feared. Every once in a while I'd jump after thinking my father was shouting to me from another room, or I'd even keep hidden for hours at a time in dark corners thinking he'd be searching for me. But after none of that happened, I was becoming more and more able to walk through the familiar hallways and various rooms with less tension in my steps.

There was one thing I still had a hard time looking at, however. Right next to the dining hall, my mother's portrait still hanged. I often found myself staring, frozen, at her chillingly similar features to mine and continuously wondering if things would be different if she hadn't died. If I hadn't killed her. And if I would be the same person I had become. It finally got to the point that I demanded her portrait be taken down and put out of sight. I could tell it upset many of the servants who'd been with the White family for many years. So many loved and admired her, but no one dared argue with me. I was the mistress of the Manor, and it helped that no one wanted to agitate me after the ordeal I'd been through.

I sat in Father's study— my study. The servants cleaned it long before my return, something I'm sure they were thrilled to do considering Father never let them touch it before. I grumbled at the paperwork before me. It was my least favorite part of running the Manor. I would much rather be reading a fairy tale or taking a stroll outside.

"Lady Snow?" Agnes, White Manor's chef, poked her ruddy head around my open door.

Lady Snow, I marveled to myself. Though that should have been my title all my life, it was never actually acknowledged.

"You can come in," I said, pushing the papers away. I was glad to have an excuse to avoid them a little longer.

Agnes stepped in with a big smile lighting up her aged face. In her hands was a plate piled with a steaming slab of white pork, and a generous serving of sweet potatoes.

"I wanted to bring you lunch myself today," she said. "We've barely seen each other or talked. Not since the night you disappeared."

I thought of that fateful night when Agnes herself was curious as to my need to cook Father an apple pie. Still, no one suspected me for his death. And that was the last I saw of Agnes before my return. Even *with* my return, we were both too busy to share more than a word or two when passing each other in the halls.

"My new responsibilities have made time for socializing difficult to come by."

Agnes nodded, chuckling. "You seem to be enjoying yourself, though."

I sighed happily and lifted my feet onto *my* desk. "I never thought life could ever be like this for me."

"None of us did." She shooed my feet away, glaring at the rising of my skirt, and put the plate in front of me. Agnes, in many ways, was like the mother I never had.

I began to dig into the food ungracefully, relishing in Agnes's cooking. I didn't realize how much I missed it until I made my return to White Manor.

"Did you hear the news?" the chef said with a grunt, displeased with my manners.

"What news?" I said around mouthfuls of pork.

"Queen Dalia and Prince Frederik set a date."

I nearly started choking. "A wedding date?"

Agnes raised an eyebrow at me. "What other 'date' could I mean? The engagement was announced nearly three months ago. It's about time."

Had that much time really gone by since the ball?

"When?" I croaked, failing to hide the turmoil I felt from my face.

Agnes studied me with her brows furrowed in concern. "Two weeks from now."

"So soon?" My breathing became ragged as the memory of Frederik's kiss ran over and over again in my mind.

"Snow, are you alright? You're awfully pale."

I lifted the back of my hand to my forehead and realized how hot I was beginning to feel.

"I'm sorry, I just realized how much work I need to do. Do you think you could leave me alone for a little while?"

I could tell she didn't believe me as she pursed her thick lips together. She hooded her eyes in suspicion, but nodded and left me alone.

"Close the door!" I called behind her.

I barely heard the door click shut as I grabbed at my pounding chest. It was happening again—that overwhelming feeling of anxiety. I didn't think I would care so much anymore about the wedding between Queen Dalia and Prince Frederik.

I rose myself from the cushions of the chair and began pacing the room frantically, scared of the tight feeling in my chest and the labored breathing. I had almost assumed that Queen Dalia would break off her engagement with the Prince after learning of his affair with me, but that didn't seem to be the case. I sprinted over to a nearby window and threw the glass pane open, hoping the fresh air from outside would help calm me, but the muggy air made things worse.

"What was I thinking?" I shouted to myself. "That one day we would find each other again, he would forgive me just like that, and we would live happily ever after?"

I dug my nails into the white wood of the windowsill.

"Idiot," I hissed aloud.

But then, realization struck me. I was never truly in the wrong. I was a parentless girl doing what she could to *survive*. There was nothing wrong with that. Even though I had lied to and manipulated Prince Frederik, there was no lie in the way I felt about him. I loved him.

No, I didn't think I would care of their impending nuptials, but I *did* care. I felt a rush of anger boil up inside of me as I thought of Queen Dalia—she was the one who ruined everything, sending her servant to reveal my true identity, and she was the one stealing my Frederik. Yes... *my* Frederik.

He was mine, and I was going to make sure no one could ever have him.

I slid my way across the thick, red carpet of the study and slammed the door open. I searched the corridors to each side of me for a roaming servant.

"You there!" I shouted to a young boy re-lighting the stifled candelabras along the wall. I'd never seen him before. He must have been new. "What's your name?"

He jumped at my beckoning and turned towards me slowly. His buggy eyes were even more prominent as he gazed at me in apprehension.

"Rothfus, m'lady."

"Do you know of any traveling gypsies, witches, warlocks, fortune tellers, anyone claiming to have magic, near here?"

He nodded quickly but still seemed confused. "Yes, my lady. There was a theatre troupe in town just yesterday, and they had a man with them doing all sorts of tricks."

"Just tricks?" I pushed. "Not real magic?"

"He was doing all sorts of mysterious things, m'lady. I saw him heal a sick dog with enchanted water for one thing."

I felt skeptical, but it was worth a shot. "Meet me outside. We leave immediately."

I started away to prepare for the trip, but the boy stood still with his head cocked to the side.

"Now!" I snapped. "Oh, and grab a few apples."

Chapter 22

Ashborne was a tiny town, more a village than anything, but it was the closest to White Manor for miles. It was often where the servants went to pick up supplies, and many had friends and family there. It also was where Father's beloved tavern, where he spent most nights, was located. I followed the serving boy as he pushed through the crowd. The smell of the common folk was putrid, almost like rotting fish.

"The troupe is set up on the edge of the square!" Rothfus shouted to me over the noise.

I merely nodded.

"Citizens of Ashborne! Come one, come all! See the amazing powers of me, the Incredible Doran, right before your eyes!"

The voice projected strongly to my ears from a reasonable distance. Rothfus leapt into a sprint, and I groaned, trying to catch up as I cursed his youthful energy.

Once we reached the large tent set in the square, probably the residence for the troupers, a tall, athletically built man came into view. He danced around in the square flamboyantly, calling an

audience to him. Most people ignored the ridiculous display, but a few curious observers trickled
over.

"The Incredible Doran!" he shouted again as he
pulled a playing card from thin air.

I grimaced. He was most likely just a trickster,
and I had just wasted an entire day. Before I could
turn to leave, however, he said something that
piqued my interest.

"Who dares to challenge my abilities? Give me
a task! Send me your sick, your bald heads, your
broken hearts... Ask your questions, know your
futures!"

A mischievous grin stretched across the man's
face, and his impossibly green eyes sparkled.

"Sir?"

A young woman with features too dull to be
pretty approached the magician. She clutched the
shoulders of an old man who seemed barely able
to stand. Doran outstretched his arms invitingly.

"Come, child," he said. "What ails him?"

"My grandfather was struck with a fever last
night, and it has not broken." The girl's voice
wavered uncontrollably. "His body isn't strong
enough to fight it. Please. He's the only family I
have left."

I found myself rising to the balls of my feet in
anticipation to see what the "Incredible Doran"
would do.

Doran stroked the long, black beard on his face,
deep in thought. He then began to nod, and the

sparkle in his eyes shone even brighter.

"I have just the thing!" he chirped.

From behind his back, he pulled out a large waterskin. Now, playing cards he could hide in his sleeve, but a waterskin? Where could he hide such a thing? The thought gave me hope that he could provide what I came for.

"Water I enchanted just a few hours ago!" he announced to the crowd. He showcased the water-skin like it was a prize horse up for auction. "Make him drink every last drop, and you will see a difference within a day." He handed the skin to the young woman, and she placed a few coins into his palm. She tearfully thanked him as the two hobbled away.

I sighed. That was hardly proof of the man's abilities. I watched as a few more people came to him with their problems and narrowed my eyes at his proclaimed "fixes."

After the crowd dispersed and Doran started counting his money with an almost scary fervor, that's when I made my move.

"Will you wait for me here, Rothfus?"

The boy started bouncing up and down. "Is it okay if I go talk to my friends, then come back?"

"Sure," I said less than warmly, waving him away. I was more focused on the task at hand.

I shouldered the satchel full of nothing but juicy, red apples and strolled over to the magician.

"The Incredible Doran, is it?" I lifted my chin with confidence and rolled my shoulders back.

He didn't even look up at me. "Show's over, miss. Come back tomorrow."

"It's Lady Snow to you," I said. This time, instead of when I was Lady Isabella, this noblewoman I portrayed was really who I had become. So beautiful it was deadly, so strong it was intimidating. But like Lady Isabella, Lady Snow had a job to do.

"Is it now?" He took the tattered hat off his head, placed his newly earned coins inside, and then slipped the hat back into place. He gave me a ridiculously exaggerated bow. "What can I do for you, *Lady Snow*."

The mocking tone he used with my title didn't faze me. "You practice real magic?"

"Who's asking?"

I rolled my eyes. "Me, of course."

He chuckled. "You're incredibly stunning, you know that?"

I tapped my fingers on my thigh impatiently. "I'm prepared to pay you *very* well if you help me." I flitted my eyes about the area. "But we must talk in private."

Doran's lips curled up into an even bigger smile than before, and he jumped high from one foot to the other.

"Oooh, I'm intrigued!" he chirruped. "Step into my office."

He gestured dramatically to the flap of the tent blowing gently in the summer breeze. I raised an eyebrow.

"Your office?"

But he ignored me and skipped away to the entrance. I followed, not nearly as enthusiastically. The inside was much larger than the outside suggested, and it was filled to the brim with elaborate costumes. My eyes watered at the abundant smells of perfumes and theatre makeup. All eyes were on me, many curious, but most looked to me in contempt. There were about a dozen players, men and women alike, with piles of dramatic makeup upon their faces. My entrance halted the practice of lines and the applying of wigs. I flushed at the sight of a man in the back in nothing but his underwear, having not been costumed yet. He merely seemed amused by my embarrassment.

Doran led me to a beautiful tapestry, elaborately designed with a sleeping lion in golden thread, much too expensive for a theatre troupe to own. But I wasn't there to judge their livelihood and decisions. The magician pushed the hanging material aside and revealed a small table with crooked legs and two rusty, metal chairs.

"Take a seat," he said, pulling out one of the chairs for me.

I obliged begrudgingly. The seat below me wobbled precariously. He sat across from me and clasped his fingers atop the table.

"Now, how may I help you?"

I opened my ears to listen from outside the tapestry and concluded that the players were making enough noise not to hear the conversation about to take place.

"What do you know about poisoned apples?"

The magician nearly fell from his chair, and he stared at me incredulously. "Who told you? Am I in trouble?"

I frowned. "Uh—"

"Was it Bavmorda? She threatened me the last time, you know!" The color was draining his face.

"Bavmorda!" I exclaimed, then lowered my voice after remembering we weren't alone. "I know her. She threatened you?"

He let out a shaky breath. "Well, Bavmorda is something of a legend among those who practice magic. But I had a rather... unpleasant encounter with her not too long ago."

I raised an eyebrow. "Were you the one she confiscated the apples from?"

He nodded and gave a nervous chuckle. "She said I was causing a lot of issues, but I don't see the harm in giving people poisoned apples. If a person wants to hurt someone else and doesn't have a deadly apple, they're just going to find a weapon anyway."

"That's..." I paused, "interesting logic."

Doran then narrowed his eyes at me. "Did she send you?"

I shook my head vehemently and gave him a charming smile. "Definitely not. I'm actually inquiring if you can provide me with this 'poison.'"

I heaved my bag of apples onto the table with a thud. The magician froze but then proceeded to laugh.

I gritted my teeth together. "Will you help me, or not?"

He placed his forearms on the table and leaned forward. "What's a pretty young thing like you going to do with poisoned apples?

"That's none of your business."

He gave me a smug smile, placing his booted feet on the table and leaning back in his chair.

"It won't be... with the right payment."

I rolled my eyes and dumped the entire contents of my coin purse on the table. He licked his lips eagerly and began counting the gold pieces.

"Money's no issue," I said. "Now help me."

He pulled the bag of apples, along with the money into his arms.

"Is two enough?" he asked.

"I believe so."

Doran clutched two pieces of fruit, one in each hand, and began chanting words I couldn't even begin to understand. His eyelids fluttered as his eyes creepily rolled to the back of his head. I turned my face away from the scene. After a few seconds, I directed my attention back to him as he placed the apples in front of me gingerly.

"One bite will only put someone in a coma," he warned.

I nodded. "And more than that is lethal. I'm aware."

He chortled at my words. "Of course you are."

"Would you like the rest of the apples?" I didn't

wait for an answer as I dumped the remaining few in front of him. He threw his hands back, startled.

"I don't want to mix up the enchanted ones with the regular," I said.

After gathering my things, I was about to leave when a thought struck me.

"Oh," I said, retaking my seat. "What can you do about disguises?"

Doran had already scooped up an apple and started munching on it as I spoke. "Like, a disguise for *you*?"

I rolled my eyes. "Yes. Can you alter my appearance? Give me a spell, or something?"

"Magic doesn't work that way."

I watched in disgust as pieces of apple stuck into Doran's thick beard. "How does it work then?"

"You can't put a spell *on* a person, per se. But you can enchant objects to *affect* people."

I rubbed my chin, deep in thought.

"I could, if you will, give you a disguise by enchanting a couple more apples." He picked another one up from the table and modeled it for me with a grin.

My eyes lit up at the thought. "Could you? It could make me look completely different?"

"For more money."

I groaned, but it was more like a growl. "I gave you everything I had with me. And it was a lot."

The man shrugged. "Do you have any valuable trinkets on you? A necklace perhaps?"

My thoughts reeled as I patted myself down in

search of something I could give him. I suddenly felt the cold hilt of Father's dagger within one of my hidden pockets— a habit I picked up after living with the boys. I hesitated before pulling it out, but there really was no dire need for it. It only ever brought on painful memories, and I could always buy a new one.

"Would this work?"

I slowly pulled out the weapon and gently placed it into Doran's palm. He studied it with a gleam in his eye. He stroked the leather handle and smiled as the steel blade glinted under the candlelight in the tent. He then quickly tucked it away and out of my sight, and it almost felt like any last connection to my father was tucked away along with it. But it wasn't sad. It was like a burden was suddenly lifted off of my shoulders. I should've gotten rid of it long ago.

Doran proceeded to grab another two apples in his hands and begin the spell, similar to before. It still made me uncomfortable to watch.

"There," he said, handing them to me. "You might want to draw on them, or something so you don't accidentally poison yourself."

I nodded at the wisdom of his words. "How do they work?"

"The more bites you take, the longer the disguise will last. But neither apple will give you any longer than a day."

"What will I look like?"

He shrugged and laughed at an internal joke.

"No idea."

Lines formed between my eyebrows. "Splendid," I said dryly.

I then nicked the two 'disguise' apples with a fingernail before placing them in the bag with the poisoned ones. Doran wiggled his fingers in an extravagant good-bye as I stood and strolled out of the tent.

"I'm excited to see what price you pay!" he called after me.

Price? I thought. Bavmorda said something like that, too... I chose to ignore the words, however. I had a job to do.

Chapter 23

I didn't tell anyone I was leaving. The servants had managed without me before, and I was convinced they would take me back once again with open arms. But if everything went according to plan, I might never have to return.

After a few days ride through uncomfortable rain and humidity, I was relieved to make it to my destination. I flipped the hood of my cloak over my head, not sure if people would recognize me as the fugitive I was. I briskly turned various corners of the city as quietly as I could. It was late enough that not a lot of people, if any, would be around. Once making it to the intended alleyway, I flicked my eyes about me, searching the night for any unwelcome spectators. Satisfied, I pressed the crumbling stone in front of me, and it clicked underneath my fingers. I stepped back as the entire wall slid back with a "whoosh."

The dining area was dark, lit only by the moon from outside, but I was left in the pitch dark as the hidden wall shut behind me. But the opening and closing of the secret entrance were loud enough to alert the boys. Within seconds, a rush of barefooted steps reached my ears as the boys bolted down the corridor. Jacob and Ben each held a candle to light the way, but the others brandished a variety of weapons to overtake their intruder.

"Hello, boys," I said with a grin.

All seven of them stood before me, weapon arms and jaws dropped in astonishment.

"Don't all greet me at once."

Looks of surprise quickly turned to anger as I was bombarded with questions and unflatteringly phrases no one should repeat. Arnold finally held his hand up to silence them all. They reluctantly obeyed.

"What do you think you're doing, Snow? After abandoning us like that?" Arnold's nostrils flared, and his entire face turned a deep red.

"It's a long story," I said.

Every single boy, down to the last little twin, folded their arms in contempt.

"You'd better start explaining, or we have no reason to not shred you to little pieces," Patrick spat, his twin brother nodding in agreement. It was hard not to laugh at the threat from the five-year-old, but I still knew he was serious.

I held up a finger and with the other hand, dug into the satchel hanging at my side. With a satisfied smile, I pulled up the string of the cloth bag I had placed in there just for that occasion. I grunted as I lifted the heavy bag, then threw it onto the floor. The drawstring flew open, and its contents spilled at the boys' feet. All eyes grew wide at the sight of the gold and jewels I brought for them.

"Is my wealth, something I'm willing to share, might I add, enough reason to keep me breathing?"

No one replied, but the rush of hands pulling up the riches and the greedy little faces were enough of an answer. All boys but one were relishing in their newfound wealth. Arnold squinted at me suspiciously.

"This is enough to travel to Lurid and then some!" Larry exclaimed.

"What do you want, Snow?" Arnold said, ignoring his brother.

I shrugged. "Nothing much. I just need somewhere to stay for the next week or so."

"Whatever for?"

With a mischievous gleam in my eye, my smile grew bigger. "I have a wedding to attend."

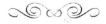

All eyes were on me as we ate breakfast. It was weird to share a meal with the seven boys and not be overwhelmed by their rambunctiousness. Though I felt wildly uncomfortable by their silence, I kept my back straight and my focus on the bowl of eggs in front of me.

"Where's Nick?"

As if they had been holding their breaths, one boy after another exhaled. They seemed to be relieved of my initiative to start a conversation.

"He's been out hunting for the last couple days," Jacob chimed in from across the table. Then, feeling satisfied with his contribution to the conversation, he pulled a book he was hiding from his lap and began to read.

"He's still around?" I asked, taking his words to mean they saw him often.

Ben, two seats to the right of me, nodded. "He figured we'd benefit from an adult influence for a while."

I raised an eyebrow. "He's taking care of you guys?"

Arnold, sitting right next to me, balled up his fists. "No! He's just helping us. Something you weren't very good at."

"Oh." I ignored the jab at me and continued shoveling the eggs into my mouth.

"He'll be back tomorrow," the twins chirped excitedly.

I almost started choking. "Really?"

The last time I saw Nick had not been pleasant. He accused me of wrongdoing, and I yelled at him for controlling me. To be fair, he was, and I had no desire to see him again.

Almost as if he was beckoned, each of us whirled around at the sound of the wall sliding back. Nick stood before us with a couple pheasants in his hand. His brown hair was disheveled, and his cheeks were hollow as if he hadn't eaten in days. He didn't seem to see me as he hung his bow and arrows on a hook in the wall and trudged his way to the table. And he *still* didn't notice as he picked up a bowl, dished up some eggs for himself, then moved to sit alone by the hearth.

The boys watched the huntsman in anticipated silence, waiting for him to see me. Arnold ruined their fun, however, by clearing his throat.

"Nick," he said. "You might want to see our visitor."

My breathing quickened as Nick's head slowly lifted to make eye contact with me.

"Hi, Snow," he said.

The boys sighed, disappointed with the less than dramatic greeting. I had to admit, I was somewhat annoyed by it myself.

"Are you not going to say anything more than that?" I snapped.

Nick nodded as he wiped some stray egg from his scruffy face. "I will. Let me eat first."

We all watched him, the boys curious, me more infuriated than anything, as he finished his breakfast. Not once did he look up at me again. Was he really that angry with me? *He* was the one in the wrong.

"Will one of you boys clean the birds like I taught you?" Nick nodded at the dead pheasants he placed on the hearth. "I'm going to talk to Snow."

He stood up stiffly and gestured for me to fol-

low him through the hall that led to the bedrooms. I pushed my chair back to oblige. Nick's
face didn't reveal any of his thoughts, but his
movements towards me were cold.

When we reached the back bedroom, the one I
stayed in over a month ago, Nick hurried me inside and slammed the door behind us. Only one
side of his face was illuminated by a single candle
in the bedroom, but I could still see the shadows
that accentuated the angles in his clenched jaw.

"How could you?" he whispered, but the words
were piercing.

"I came back, didn't I?"

He shot me an icy glare, and I felt myself shiver.
"Those poor boys *depended* on you!"

"I was *scared*!" I shouted back.

Nick took two steps back, but he still seemed
angry with me. After a pause that felt to last an
eternity, he finally seemed to relax.

"Are you okay?"

I rolled my shoulders back and stared back at
him confidently. "Don't give me your sympathy. I
don't regret anything."

Nick's brows drew together, and he looked as if
he was about to shout at me again. He clenched
and unclenched his fists about a dozen times, and
then a shadow of determination flashed across his
face. He charged me, a very similar approach to
what Father had done to me time and time again.
But instead of hitting me, Nick grabbed my arms
and crushed me against his chest. He hesitated

for a moment, face hovered above my own, and before I could process what was happening, he pressed his lips against mine— hard.

I gasped and pushed him away with all my strength and hurried myself to the other side of the room.

"How dare you?" I cried.

And with that, I turned briskly on my heel and stormed away. I didn't even care to look back, but I could feel his hungry, yearning eyes boring into my back.

Chapter 24

I demanded no one to bother me. Disregarding whether or not my old room was available, I shacked up in there for a little over a week and prepared myself for my visit with Queen Dalia. I only ever left for a bite or two eat every day, or to relieve myself.

Someone knocked.

"That better be you, Arnold!" I shouted.

Arnold turned the knob and precariously craned his head around the door. "You needed me, Snow?"

I nodded fervently and waved for him to come in. "I need your help."

He raised an eyebrow. "With what?"

"Do you know how secure the servants' entrance at the castle is?"

Arnold plopped down onto my cot with a sigh. "Snow, what are you planning?"

"Is it?" I was losing my patience.

Arnold flinched slightly at my sharp words. "Not really. Not at certain times, especially."

My eyes widened with curiosity. "What times?"

"In the mornings. They usually get their food

and other supply deliveries a little after dawn every day. Many servants are always out and about to help load it all in."

I suppressed the urge to bounce up and down. "Where is the servants' entrance?"

He folded his arms. "I'm not telling you unless you explain what's going on."

I folded my arms, as well. "It's my business."

Arnold leapt from his seat and stared me down. "Then I'm at least coming with you."

I laughed. "Do you really care about my safety?"

"Snow!" he said, exasperated. "Yes, we were angry when you didn't come back, but we were mostly..." He shifted his gaze to the floor. "We were worried about you, alright?"

I exhaled through my nose loudly. "Fine. You can come with me. We leave at first light tomorrow morning."

It was the day of the royal wedding, and I was determined— excited, even. I studied myself in the full-length mirror in my bedroom, trying to determine if the plain dress Arnold had found me would be servant-y enough. The tan cloth fell baggily over my shoulders and looked a little worn at the hem. It would do.

I fingered a knife in yet another hidden pocket Arnold sewed into the dress for me. The twins lent me one of their "less important knives—" their words— since I sold Father's dagger. It was a duller blade, in more ways than one, but it would do.

"You know there's probably still a look-out for you, right?"

Arnold was standing behind me dressed in his own serving clothes of worn trousers and a plain tunic.

"Hand me the sack sitting on the bed, will you?"

He opened his mouth to protest my refusal to reply to his question, but changed his mind and grabbed the sack for me. I pulled out one of the apples, feeling around the skin to find the nick I made to determine it from the poisoned ones.

"You just ate breakfast," he said.

I ignored him again and took a bite. Some of the juice dripped down my chin, and I eyed the white interior appreciatively. It was a good apple. I proceeded to finish the entire piece of fruit, then looked curiously into the mirror. Nothing happened.

"Uh… Snow, you're scaring me."

"Ugh," I shouted, throwing the core to the floor. "It didn't work!"

But in that moment my long, dark hair faded into a brilliant gold, and my skin tanned to an appealing bronze. My waist thickened out ever so slightly, and my height even shrunk an inch or two. The only things that stayed the same were the distinctive red of my lips and my brown eyes.

Arnold had apparently run over to the edge of the room in fright during my transformation. His nails were digging into the wall, and his legs trembled beneath him.

"What— what— Oh my," he stammered.

I laughed at his reaction. "You'd think a half-dwarf wouldn't be so surprised by a little magic."

Arnold gulped.

"What did you tell your brothers about our excursion?"

His teeth chattered, and it took a second or two for him to regain his composure. "Nothing much. I just told them not to wait up for us— that you were helping me with another job."

"And Nick? Did he say anything?" He and I hadn't spoken since that kiss. We were both avoiding each other, not even making eye contact as we passed during meals or in the hall.

"He hasn't even acknowledged that anything is happening. Besides, he left for another hunting trip yesterday."

"Oh, I didn't notice," I said, and I found that I didn't really care. "Is everybody still asleep?"

Arnold nodded. He still stared at me, but instead of fright in his eyes, it slowly became wonder.

"Off we go then."

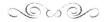

Arnold gestured for me to crouch down and follow him towards one of the three delivery carts at
the side of the castle. A horde of servants had already started picking up various parcels, food, and
supplies from the carts.

"How much stuff does one place need?" I muttered as we hid behind a cart and out of sight.

"Alright, Snow," Arnold whispered. "Act really
casual and follow my lead."

Careful to see no one was looking our way, Arnold stood up and briskly stepped around the cart
to pick up his own parcel. I did the same.

"You there!" someone yelled at me.

My heart jumped to my throat as I whirled
around to the owner of the voice. A tall, burly man
stood at the edge of the cart and glared down at
me.

"You can do better than that."

I furrowed my brow, trying to decipher what he
was referring to, then looked down at the parcel in
my arms. It was very small, and I noticed the rest
of the crowd around me carried stacks of supplies
each.

"Oh." I gave him a wry smile. "Sorry."

The man dropped another two packages on top
of the one. The string tying the parcels together

scratched at my arms, and the shapes were so awkward, but I hid my discomfort.

"Snow," Arnold hissed next to me. "Let's move."

We fell into place at the end of the long line leading to the double-doored servants' entrance.

"This is going to take a while," I grumbled.

"Just act natural."

"Arnold." I elbowed him slightly in the ribs but immediately regretted it as I was forced to rebalance my tipping packages. "I excel at this stuff, remember?"

He merely grunted in return.

After a good half hour, we finally made it into the kitchens and were directed to place our packages in an endlessly growing pile.

"Where do you need to go?" Arnold whispered to me.

"Now *you* follow *my* lead."

I surveyed the enormous kitchens around us and squinted at the heat radiating from one of the large ovens directly to my right. There was an organized chaos as one chef after another bustled about in preparation for the wedding feast that night. Being so close to the wedding preparations made me angry all over again. I needed to hurry.

We pushed past the multitude, getting a couple, "Watch it!"s and one or two, "Hey!"s. After reaching the end of the kitchen, I noticed a tray with a couple spools of thread and a thimble and needle. My brain started working double-time as I thought of how I could put those to use and shoved them into a hidden pocket.

"What do you need those for?" Arnold asked.

"We'll see."

I swung the door in front of us open and strode confidently into the adjoining hallway. It was a much smaller space than the hall Nick, and I had traversed when attending the ball, but the carpeting and tapestried walls were still magnificent. Arnold whistled, and I realized it was his first time in the castle.

"Come on," I said.

I quickened my pace when I saw a young serving maid dusting a bust at the end of the corridor. She looked to be about my age and was humming an unfamiliar tune.

"Excuse me?" I said.

The girl jumped, nearly falling off her stool at the fright. "Oh, goodness me. You scared me half to death, you did."

I gave her an apologetic smile, but before I could continue with my question, Arnold interrupted me.

"Who's that a bust of?"

"The late King, lad." The girl looked at the figure sadly. "Died so young, he did."

I suppressed an eye roll. "Excuse me, but I'm new here, and the royal seamstress requested I take a final look at the Queen's wedding dress." I help up the thimble and needle for her to see. "I assume the dress is already with Her Majesty? Would you know?"

"Oh, yes. I saw them deliver it myself. Wait 'til you see it!" Her eyes glowed from the memory.

"Where are her rooms? Like I said, I'm new."

The maid glanced at Arnold next to me. "He's coming with you to the Queen's rooms?"

"Oh, no." I made myself chuckle. "Arnold's new, too. He just wanted to explore a little bit with me on the way. He won't assist me." I nudged Arnold playfully, and he joined me in the feigned laughter.

"Of course. Two flights up from here, third chamber on your right." She smiled sweetly. "Maybe you can find me later and let me know what you thought about her dress."

I nodded, but my feet kept shifting from one to another with impatience. As the girl finally returned to her dusting, I grabbed Arnold's arm and pulled him to the staircase next to us. The mahogany of the stairs was so fantastically polished to create a brilliant shine, I was afraid I would slip on them. After a careful couple of steps, I determined there was no danger of such a thing and began my ascension. The railing was smooth under my touch and shimmered with hints of gold in its wood-work. If I hadn't been there for a particular purpose, I might've taken more time to admire the castle décor.

It seemed Arnold didn't sense the urgency as he took a moment to study every portrait along his path.

"Arnold!" I snapped. "Are you coming, or not?"

"Sorry," he breathed. "I've just never seen anything so *amazing.*"

He reluctantly caught up to me, and we began our trek up the second flight of stairs. We finally reached yet another corridor, but this one was adorned with chamber doors rather than por-traits and tapestries.

"One, two, three," I counted aloud. "Here it is." The big door was simple, but elegant at the same time with its flattering, brown varnish.

"I'll wait out here for you," Arnold whispered, but he wrung his hands together nervously. "Why exactly do you need to see the Queen?"

"I just have something to give her," I replied.

Before Arnold could say anything more, I knocked confidently on the wood and listened for a voice calling me in. It came, and I took a deep breath as I placed my hand on the door handle. This was it. I pushed the door open and plastered a kind smile on my face, but hunched my shoul-ders ever so slightly and urged a reddening to my cheeks to present a demure servant.

Queen Dalia stood before a full-length mirror that seemed to be more silver than glass. She twirled back and forth, staring at her figure in the reflection. The dress she wore had a tight bodice that ended and flared at her hips into a skirt bigger than I'd ever seen. Silver beading stretched across the silky fabric in ways that only a royal seam-stress could accomplish. The Queen's long, red hair shone against the white of her gown starkly — something I would have thought would be un-flattering, but it worked so well that I felt a stab of jealousy tremor inside of me.

I tried to push the feelings away to announce my presence. "Your Majesty, you look stunning." And I found that I meant it.

"Ugh!" the Queen groaned. "It's too large in the bust. No matter what I say, it seems the seamstresses are keen on thinking my chest is larger than it really is."

Queen Dalia threw herself onto her bed, a pile of white surrounding her like a mountain. Then she sat bolt upright and eyed me curiously.

"Why are you here? I've never seen you before."

I cleared my throat, but every part of my body stayed firm. The nerves only added to the thrill I felt by being there. I held up the thimble and needle for her to see.

"I'm new, but the seamstress sent me to make sure your wedding dress was fitting you well."

The Queen rolled her eyes. "Well, it's not," she spat.

I took a couple steps back in shock at her tone.

She sighed. "I'm so sorry. I'm just a little...nervous." She started pleating her skirts mindlessly with her fingers.

I nodded. "That's perfectly understandable, Your Majesty. Let me take a look at your dress."

The Queen moved to stand once again, and I stepped over in her direction. But out of the corner of my eye, I saw something black. Startled, I whirled to see what it was. Before me was *another* mirror, resting atop the vanity mirror (How many mirrors did this girl need?), but it was more regal-looking than the full-length one the Queen stood in front of. The twists and curves of the golden frame were incredible, but that's not what caught my eye. Before me was my reflection— my *normal* reflection! Ebony hair and fair skin presented itself within the glass. I grabbed at the hair on top of my head. It was still blonde, but why... and then my reflection smiled. I gasped, touching my lips. I hadn't smiled.

"Are you coming?" the Queen interrupted me from my reverie.

I moved quickly away from the mysterious mirror and looked at Queen Dalia nervously, but she was still studying her gown. I released a sigh of relief. She hadn't noticed. But why did the Queen have what seemed to be an enchanted mirror?

I shook my head. There was no time for questions. I needed to finish what I came for and get out of there.

"Do you see where it gaps up here in the front?" The Queen pointed to the fabric below her collarbone.

I nodded, rubbing my chin. I had no knowledge of sewing and measuring, but I did my best to pretend in measuring her with my hands and taking mental notes. She seemed convinced.

"Alright, Your Majesty. I will go tell the seamstress right away what needs to be done with the dress. I'll send her up here immediately."

I then grabbed the Queen's arm and moved her to sit back on the bed.

"You look incredibly pale," I said, trying to hold in the giggles coming from the excitement I felt bubbling up inside of me.

Queen Dalia nodded, taking deep breaths and exhaling loudly.

"You should really eat something," I pressed, rummaging through the cloth bag at my side. After feeling the skin of the apples within its contents, I found one without a nick in it.

"Here," I continued, holding it out to her. I made my brows furrow together, drawing worry lines into my forehead. "Even just a couple bites of something. We don't want you fainting at the ceremony."

The Queen eyed the fruit in my hands skeptically, but I soon saw her features relax in resolve. "You're right."

My finger trembled slightly, almost revealing my eagerness as she picked the apple from my outstretched palm. I tried to keep my lips from twitching into a smile as Queen Dalia ran her fingers along the apple.

"Thank you," she whispered.

"Go on now," I urged, getting a little impatient.

The Queen's pink lips hovered over the apple, her white teeth gleaming as she was about to puncture the skin. Seconds began to tick by slowly as I leaned forward on my toes, waiting eagerly for that crunch, but a knock on the door interrupted it from happening. Queen Dalia put her arm down and rested the apple on her mattress, quickly forgetting about it.

"Will you see who that is?" the Queen asked gently.

I curtsied, but my nostrils flared, and my hands shook from annoyance. Moving to the door, I muttered under my breath.

I'll just have to remind her to eat it, I told myself.

As soon as I turned the knob, a tall young woman burst through, pushing me to the floor. I couldn't even see who it was through the flurry of movement. I bit my tongue as the push caused me to stub my toe against the wall.

"Leave us!" the woman snapped at me.

With a better look than before, I gasped as I recognized the face. It was that lady-in-waiting. The one the Queen had sent to reveal my identity to the Prince and ruin everything. I frowned and looked at the Queen for her orders.

Queen Dalia waved me away. "It's okay. Just send the seamstress here as soon as you can."

My heart sank to my stomach with a painful thud. She'd forgotten about the apple. And even if she did eat it, I wouldn't be there to witness the satisfying scene of her body twisting in pain until her life ended.

With a final attempt before leaving the room, I shouted, "Be sure to eat that apple, Your Majesty! You need it."

Chapter 25

"Who was that?" Aeryn asked, jumping on the bed next to her Queen.

Dalia shrugged. "An apprentice to the seamstress, maybe? She said she was new."

Aeryn whistled as she finally moved her gaze to the gown upon Queen Dalia. "Oh, my. It's *beautiful*!"

Dalia grimaced. "It's too big on my chest."

"It is?" Aeryn cocked her head to the side. "I didn't even notice."

Standing proved to take a great effort for the Queen as she pushed the skirts out of her way.

"What's really bothering you?" Aeryn asked, concern leaking through her voice.

Dalia paced around the room, wringing her hands together. "You'll just laugh at me."

Her lady-in-waiting lifted a hand in promise. "I won't. I swear."

Dalia sighed. "I keep thinking that The Fairest will somehow ruin everything. That she'll turn up and steal the Prince away."

Aeryn snorted but stopped after receiving a disapproving glare from the Queen. She cleared her throat.

"Dalia, that woman hasn't been seen for a *month*. And even if she wanted to show up, I'm positive the threat of guards and soldiers who now know of her plight would scare her well enough away."

"Still," Dalia said as she determinedly strolled over to her magic mirror.

"Dalia, it's pointless. You'll just keep worrying if you continue to spy on her. Ooh," Aeryn was interrupted by the sight of the apple beside her. "Were you going to eat this?"

"Go ahead," Dalia said, barely paying attention. "Mirror, mirror on the wall—"

"You're going to do it anyway?" Aeryn asked as she crunched through the apple. "Wow, this is *delicious*!" She took another bite.

"Mirror, mirror on the wall," Dalia started again, "show me the fairest one of all."

The glass turned to liquid and swirled with its usual flashes of light before fading into an image of a pretty, modest girl with golden hair.

"Wait," Dalia said. "That's the servant that was just in here!"

Aeryn didn't answer, but Dalia continued to squint at the image.

"That's so weird... Did The Fairest die, or something? Or maybe the mirror decided someone else is the most beautiful in the land?"

Dalia's eyes scanned over the woman in the glass as she walked down the castle halls with a shorter boy at her side. She was pretty, but hardly the *fairest*. Dalia thought of her own features, the brilliant red hair and fine figure. Surely *she* was prettier than this girl. Dalia continued watching, then gasped as Prince Frederik turned the corner and halted in front of the maiden. A look of recognition flashed across his blue eyes but went away just as quickly as it had come. He shook his head as if confused, then bowed and excused himself. The maiden grabbed his arm as he passed and whispered something in his ear. His eyes grew wide, and he kept opening and closing his mouth as if to say something.

Dalia watched, stiff and in horror, as he followed the servant out of sight. And just like that, the image faded away and returned to Dalia's reflection.

"What—what— I'm so confused!" Dalia stammered, throwing herself onto the chair at the vanity. "What could she say to make the Prince look so intrigued and follow her like that?"

Her thoughts churned violently as she tried to explain what she had just seen to herself, but then realization struck her like a bolt of lightning.

"Aeryn!" she cried. "Don't eat that apple!"

Dalia leapt from her chair and pushed through her cumbersome gown to make it to her friend, but she was too late. Aeryn's cold body was sprawled across the Queen's mattress, nothing but emptiness in her stormy eyes.

"Guards," Dalia croaked through the hot tears

that suddenly sprang from her eyes. "Guards!" she cried, louder this time. "How could she? How *could* she?"

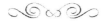

"Come on, Arnold," I hissed. "We have to hurry. Before they catch us."

Arnold flashed me a nervous glance. "What did you do?"

I shook my head. "Nothing yet. It's what *might* happen."

We stepped, nearly sprinted through the hallways towards the staircase. I could be in a *lot of trouble* if we didn't get out of there quickly. I grumbled to myself. It could have gone much better, and I felt my head reel at the thought that I might've failed. I hoped I *didn't* fail... Queen Dalia deserved what I was trying to do. She had stolen Frederik from me.

As if my thoughts of him called him to me, I skidded to a halt as Prince Frederik turned the corner and was heading directly towards us.

Noticing that I had stopped, Arnold retraced his own steps and followed where my eyes were.

"Who's that?" he whispered.

"It's him," I breathed. My heart was skipping beats.

Arnold's eyes grew wide. "Prince Frederik? Come on!" He tried to pull me away, but I stood firmly in place, mesmerized by the Prince's presence.

Frederik halted himself and met my eyes. A flash of recognition lit up his face, and it startled him so much that he stumbled two steps backward. Did he know it was me? But he quickly moved his gaze away from me and shook his head, as if convincing himself otherwise. He began to walk past me, but without thinking, I grabbed his arm and squeezed, as if trying to determine if he really was there.

He looked down at me again, brows furrowed in confusion. "Do I know you from somewhere?"

"Frederik," I whispered. "It's me."

This time recognition turned to astonishment as Frederik's eyes bulged out of his head.

"Why are you here? And why do you look like that?" he said through gritted teeth. But he seemed more nervous than angry with me. That gave me hope.

"Can we talk somewhere?"

His eyes flitted about the area, but he gave me a curt nod. I led him away from the corridor in hopes to find a secluded corner.

"I guess I'll just stay here." Arnold shifted from foot to foot nervously.

I ignored him. My thoughts were only on Frederik. A door to the left of us was wide open and rather dark inside. Frederik pulled me inside after looking back and forth for any onlookers for the hundredth time. He shut the door behind us.

"This is my room," he told me.

I looked around. There was a four-poster bed, not as tall and decorated as the Queen's, but still luxurious, and a large throw rug of a forest green stretched under our feet. Across from us was a quaint bay window with the curtains drawn. Just a small sliver of sunlight shone into the room. Frederik's eyes followed where mine rested.

"Ah. Should I open the curtains?"

He moved to do so, but I grabbed his hand to stop him. "No. We don't want anyone from outside to see, either."

Frederik once again eyed me incredulously. "How did you get here, Isabella? And how do you look like *that*?" He looked me up and down once again, the line between his brows growing deeper and deeper. "I will say, though. Your eyes are still the same. That's how I was able to recognize you."

"Snow, remember? And about my disguise, it's a long story. I was hoping to see you." I thrust my hands into his and squeezed tightly. I could feel him tense, but he didn't pull away. He didn't say anything, so I continued:

"Frederik." I heard him draw in a sharp breath. "I'm so sorry for lying to you. I was just trying to survive. You have no idea what I've been through."

"Snow…" he whispered. "I can't."

A storm of fury began to overwhelm me. "Why not?" I hissed. "Do you love *her*?"

He winced at the way I referred to the Queen, but then said, "I love *you*."

I pulled myself closer to the Prince and craned my neck up to his face. "Then run away with me. Like you said."

I couldn't see his eyes very well in the dim lighting, but as he replied, his voice wavered as if he was starting to get emotional.

"I can't."

Tears of my own sprung from my eyes, and I pushed myself away. "But you love me."

His head was lowered to the floor, and his breathing became ragged. "I'm sorry."

At that very moment, the door burst open, and an entourage of five or six guards dressed in blue and white circled around me, swords pointed threateningly in my direction. Frederik seemed surprised, but he stepped out of their way.

"Frederik," I cried. "help me!"

He wouldn't reach my gaze.

"You're under arrest," one of the guards barked. He was dressed finer than his companions, perhaps the captain of the guard.

I struggled against one of the men who was tying my arms behind my back. "Frederik!" I shouted again, but it was pointless.

Chapter 26

I rocked back on my knees with my hands clutching the iron bars in front of me. I felt horribly exposed after the guards had searched me and taken away everything in my pockets, including the knife and even the needle and thimble. My hair was already starting to change to its normal black. The disguise had only lasted for a few hours, even though I ate the entire apple. Stupid magician. But that didn't matter now.

I studied my surroundings and crinkled up my nose in displeasure. There was a certain rank to the dungeons, like rotten eggs and body odor, that made my eyes water. The cells around me seemed to have no end, but most of them were empty. A few cell blocks down from mine was a scrawny old man with rotten teeth and dirt covering every inch of his body. His beady eyes did not leave my figure as he grinned. I almost gagged.

"Hey!" I shouted, shaking the bars. "Is anyone there?"

After having been roughly thrown into the prison, every last guard left me by myself. I was sure they had someone stationed nearby, though.

I needed answers, like what they were planning to do with me. And where was Arnold? He must've abandoned me when the first sign of trouble appeared. I didn't blame him. I would've done the same.

Footsteps sounded a short distance away from me, and I pressed my face against the cold bars to try and get a better look in the darkness. The man I had assumed to be captain of the guard strolled over to my cell with a blank look on his face. Trailing behind him was the Queen. I cursed under my breath. She was still alive. Prince Frederik was with her and grasping her shoulders in comfort. For a split second, we made eye contact, but he quickly turned his face away.

"The Queen tells me your name is Snow," the guard said as he dropped to my level, but still a safe distance from my cell. The large muscles in his arms pulsed from the strain. Where there once was a blank look, an eager smile started to grow on his face. "I'm the captain of the guard, Sir Derrik."

So, I was right about his title. I glared back, refusing to give him the satisfaction of a reply.

Sir Derrik pulled a small knife from his boot and began stroking the blade fondly. "The Queen *also* tells me you've done some pretty despicable things, my dear."

My knuckles were beginning to turn white as I gripped the bars. Sir Derrik studied the scowl on my face and merely laughed.

"First, you stole things, then you took advantage of Prince Frederik, and now you tried to kill your Queen."

I looked at Frederik, and all the color drained from his face. It seemed this was the first he heard of my attempting murder on his fiancée, but I remained silent.

The guard ran the tip of his knife along the bars, nearly meeting the blade with my fingers. "Do you deny these claims?"

Why wasn't the Queen saying anything to me? I studied her huddled figure as she sobbed into Frederik's chest. His arms were around her. I clenched my teeth.

"Your Majesty?" Sir Derrik turned to Queen Dalia. "Do you have the apple with you?"

The Queen hiccupped and nodded, then pulled out a half-eaten apple hidden in her grip, handed it to the guard, then returned to her pathetic position against Frederik.

I stared, confused, at the apple as the guard rolled it in his hand. There were bites taken out of it. Who had bitten into it? Who had died? Obviously not my intended victim...

"You're awfully quiet, Snow. You know, I did some digging. A certain Lord White of White Manor had a daughter named Snow, but he died — presumably from poison. And then his daughter disappeared at about the same time." He eyed me, licking his lips. "Did you have something to do with Lord White's death, Snow?"

My eyes didn't waver from his dark brown.

"Eat it," he said, holding it out to me through the bars.

Out of reflex, I jumped back and paled. He chuckled again.

"Ah, so you do know this apple is deadly."

"No," I finally said. "I've never seen it before!"

"Snow…" he clicked his tongue. "We have witnesses. And Queen Dalia says a young serving maid with golden hair gave this apple to her." He licked his lips again. "And I, myself, watched *you* turn from that woman into what you are now. Quite the trick, might I add, disguising yourself. How did you do it?"

For the first time, I shifted my gaze away from him.

"Eat it," he said. "I have a feeling that if you truly are innocent of attempted murder, this apple won't kill you. If you're not… well, my job of killing you myself will get a lot easier."

I eyed the fruit in his hand as the juices dripped from the few bites already punctured in its skin. I racked my brain for something, anything I could do to get out of eating the apple. But then my eyes fell to his other hand. The knife in his grip was pointed directly at me, and the blade gleamed as if eager to taste my blood. I gulped. There was no way out of it. But there was one small glimmer of hope…

If I just eat one bite, I thought, *I won't actually die.*

"If I eat it, and something happens to me," I

whispered, "will you promise to find a man named Nicholas Smith?"

"If something happens to you?" The guard smirked. "You're saying you know the apple is poisonous?"

"I'm not saying that!" I spat. "But obviously you are scared of it for some reason, and I want someone I know to have my body if something happens."

The guard raised an eyebrow. "I'll make no promises."

"It's alright," Frederik chimed in. "I think everyone deserves a proper burial surrounded by people who care about them." He directed his gaze to me. "I'll make sure it happens, Snow. *If* something happens to you." He put a lot of strain on the word "if."

So, the Prince had hope that this apple wouldn't do anything to me— That everybody was mistaken about my intentions. I found myself smiling. Maybe, if Nick and the boys could figure out that I wasn't actually dead, they would be able to find a way to revive me. Frederik's worried look gave me even more hope that maybe there was still a chance for the two of us, as well.

I expected the Queen to be angry at Frederik's promise to me, but she was still shaking from her sobs.

I snatched the apple from the guard's hand and without hesitation, took a single bite. It was delicious. I could almost taste the death laced within its juices, and it was an intoxicating, thrilling flavor. I threw the apple away from myself and awaited the indefinite sleep that was to overtake me. The last things I remembered were the sobs of the Queen, the look of horror from Frederik, and the gleeful chuckles of the guard.

Chapter 27

Queen Dalia was shaking uncontrollably in the Prince's arms. He tried to avoid looking at the lifeless body of Isabe—Snow and focused on comforting his betrothed. He rubbed his hands along her arms and whispered comforting words.

"She killed— she killed Aeryn," she stammered.

The words struck Frederik like a knife to the heart. Snow really had been a killer. He didn't want to believe it, but it was true.

"Maybe we should postpone the wedding," Frederik whispered.

Queen Dalia nodded quickly. "I think that's best," she said. "I'm so sorry."

"No," he reassured her. "*Terrible* things have happened today."

Sir Derrik rose from his position in front of Snow's cell and unlocked her door. He then strode over to the Prince. He bowed, but the look of disapproving in his face was evident to Frederik.

"I would suggest getting rid of the body quickly, Your Highness," he said coldly. "Or I'll dispose of it myself. My way."

Frederik shivered, getting the impression that

the captain of the guard was a violent man who enjoyed the suffering of others.

"Don't worry. I will."

"Your Majesty," Derrik directed to Dalia. "May I escort you back to your rooms?"

She nodded, lip trembling. "Is Aeryn... Is she...?"

"She's been moved."

Their voices were fading further and further away as they left the dungeons. Frederik stalked over to Snow's cell and pulled the door open quietly, as if she were merely sleeping and he was afraid to wake her. Frederik looked around the room to see if there were any other prisoners or guards around. There was just one sickly-looking man a few cells down, but he had a crazed look in his eye as he muttered incomprehensible things and whittled away at the floor with a piece of straw.

Frederik's eyes fell to the body at his feet. She really was beautiful. More so than any other woman he'd ever seen. Her ebony hair stretched across the stone floor like a dark waterfall, and a touch of pink adorned her soft cheekbones. She really did look like she was just sleeping. He then found himself staring at her blood-red lips. They were parted ever so slightly as if witty words were about to spill from them, something she had always done. He was mesmerized by her mouth and felt drawn to it.

Frederik dropped to his knees and was unable

to fight the urge to kiss her just one last time. He leaned forward, eyes closed...

"I wouldn't do that if I were you."

Frederik leapt up from the ground, startled by the unfamiliar voice. Before him was an impossibly old, impossibly *ugly* woman with a balding head and strong smell. She sat on the sill of the small, barred window in front of him and kicked her feet back and forth like a little girl. How did she get up there? Better yet, how did she get in there without him noticing?

"Who are you?"

The woman rolled her eyes. "I *hate* this part, so don't interrupt me." She took a deep breath. "I'm Bavmorda. A witch? Yes, I'm a witch. But don't worry, I'm not going to hurt you. I can help. And please... no questions." She eyed him, daring him to defy her request.

Frederik gulped. "Okay." He knew of the existence of sorcery and witches, so it was definitely possible one could pop up wherever she pleased.

"Okay?" Bavmorda looked shocked, then relaxed. "Good. Great." She leapt from the window more gracefully than a woman of her age should've been able to.

"As I was saying," she continued. "Don't kiss her."

Frederik blushed slightly. "How do you know I was going to kiss her?"

Bavmorda raised an eyebrow, then started chuckling. "Well, it didn't look like you were going to hit her!"

The Prince opened his mouth to object, but she was right.

"Anyway, please don't do it. Your love for her is strong enough to awaken her."

Frederik stumbled backward. "She's still alive?"

"Mmm..." She shifted her head from side to side. "More or less."

Frederik looked to Snow again, incredulous. "How can that be? Is Aeryn—"

Bavmorda interrupted. "The Queen's servant took more than one bite, I'm assuming."

"But—"

Bavmorda raised a hand to silence him. "Long story."

There was a long pause before Frederik spoke again. "Why do you think I love her so?"

The witch placed her hands on her hips and pursed her cracked lips, thinking. "Snow White has not had the chance to grow into the person she has the potential to be. A kind, loving soul. I believe it has a lot to do with her terrible father."

Frederik was about to try another question, but he thought not to press the issue.

"I think you were able to see the good that's inside her. It also helps that she's a looker." Bavmorda clicked her tongue at Snow. "Too bad she's a little insane."

"What do we do now, though? If she's still alive? We can't just *bury* her, can we?"

Bavmorda cackled. "Oh no, child." She approached the Prince and patted him comfortingly on the shoulder. He flinched at the mysterious woman's closeness. "I'll take her somewhere safe. Somewhere that one day, I might give her a second chance."

Frederik wiped his clammy hands against his trousers. "What about me? Can't I help her?"

Bavmorda was already lifting Snow into her arms, another incredible feat for such an old woman. She shook her head sternly at the Prince.

"You two walk different paths," she said. "Try it out with the Queen."

"But—"

"Frederik!" Bavmorda scolded him like a child. "I promise you that with time, you could learn to love Dalia. She's a wonderful person and needs someone in this dark time of her life. That could be you, if she decides that. And if she does, I would be grateful if I were you."

Frederik skeptically folded his arms. "How do you know all this?"

The woman groaned. "Did you *not* listen to my speech about being a witch?"

The Prince looked back down at his love and felt a pang in his heart as it broke. After about a minute, he came to a resolution.

"Take care of her," he whispered. "I want her to have that second chance."

Bavmorda's face softened, and she smiled. "I will."

And with that, she disappeared, with Snow in

her arms, just as quickly as she had come.

Chapter 28

The Kingdom of Lurid, Bavmorda's old home. It had barely changed. The rolling hills and the smell of pine brought back a rush of memories, both good and bad. She stared at the mountains she was climbing and felt her heart warm from hiking them again. But in that moment, she had a purpose. She always had a purpose. And helping others was always the most significant part of those "purposes."

She glanced down at the face of the young woman in her arms. Snow White. Hair as black as ebony, skin as white as snow, lips the color of blood... What trouble she had caused. Bavmorda shook her head in disdain. It wasn't all her fault, though. Snow's mother died and left her with a malicious father. Snow's mind must've slowly destroyed itself until her perspective of the world, and the people around her were warped.

Bavmorda grunted as she shifted the girl's weight and trudged onward through the cold air. Where did those blasted dwarves lodge themselves again? She muttered a location spell under her breath and was relieved to see they weren't far.

She followed the new trail of light from her spell resting upon the white snow at her feet. Within the next few minutes, Bavmorda approached the familiar cave she had taken shelter in all those years ago— *many* years ago.

She rushed into the warmth of a large fire burning inside and rested Snow onto the cave floor gently. A tiny man, not any taller than four feet, hobbled towards her with a pick-ax resting on his shoulder.

"Bavmorda?" he exclaimed. "Is that you?" His bushy red eyebrows and long beard made it hard to see his expression, but he seemed thrilled to see her.

Bavmorda smiled. "Tulmaic, it's so good to see you again."

He rushed over as quickly as his short legs could muster and hugged her around the knees. "You look the same!"

She chuckled. "Always have. You don't look much different, yourself."

He patted his round stomach jovially. "I sure have grown width-wise, mind you."

The two old friends laughed together for another few minutes, but then Bavmorda was reminded of the task at hand.

"I need your help," she said. "Do you know of a safe place I can put her? Maybe somewhere no one will find her until I want them to?"

Tulmaic jumped back as if noticing the maiden at his feet for the first time. "What's wrong with her?"

Bavmorda waved the words away. "Oh, she's just sleeping. For a long time."

He raised an eyebrow. "Enchanted, eh? You always had a knack for being around that sort of thing."

"Can you help me?"

He scratched his chin. "I might know of a place. A very secluded part of the forest way past the mountain chain."

The witch nodded. "That's perfect."

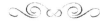

Bavmorda walked alongside Tulmaic. They traveled for a few days, on foot, but she didn't complain. She missed journeys among the mountains, and dwarves had their own inhuman endurance, so Tulmaic didn't complain, either. Trailing behind them were a couple more of Tulmaic's dwarven brothers. They carried Snow within a beautiful glass coffin.

"Where did you get a coffin like that?" Bavmorda asked.

Tulmaic shrugged. "We made it."

"For what purpose?"

"Sometimes we like to experiment." He threw a look back at the beautiful maiden within the glass box. "And someone as pretty as that still deserves to be seen." He looked at Bavmorda wryly. "Even if it's just you, as it seems you've been implying."

Bavmorda smirked but didn't reply.

"This is it," Tulmaic said.

Bavmorda spun around to take in their surroundings: a small clearing hidden tightly away by a thick line of tall pine trees. A thin layer of fine snow crunched under her steps. A perfect place for her maiden to rest—lying upon the white snow.

"Put her in the middle there."

The other dwarves heaved the glass box past her and gingerly placed it where Bavmorda pointed.

"These woods are *weeks* away from any settlement," Tulmaic explained to her. "So no one should be able to find her."

"Especially not with some enchantments, they won't," Bavmorda chirped.

Tulmaic's belly bounced as he chuckled. "We'll leave you to it, then."

"Wait, before you go. Seven little boys are living in the heart of Edristan's capital," Bavmorda said. "Their father was your brother, Udril. They're orphans, and I think they would benefit greatly from your help."

Tulmaic's eyes grew wide. "I knew he had children, but..." He shook his head, not wanting to face painful memories. "Thank you for telling me. We'll make sure those boys are taken care of and brought to Lurid."

Bavmorda nodded, then shooed them away so she could do her spells. After the last dwarf hobbled away from the clearing, Bavmorda stretched out her arms and shouted the words to the spell that would create an enchanted border around the glass coffin.

"There," she said to herself. "That should keep people out. Until I allow the right person to come in."

She moved her attention to the sleeping maiden. A price must always be paid for the use of magic to harm others, and there was the proof.

"You'll get another chance, Snow," she whispered. "Let's allow your heart to heal for a while."

Epilogue

100 Years Later...

This had to be the place that witch was talking about. I had never seen it before. The tall pines around me were almost impossible to get through. The snow before me in the clearing was slowly beginning to melt away, beckoning spring. Even a flower or two popped out from hiding. But that was not what held my gaze. Right in front of me was a box— a coffin, maybe— and every last inch of it was made out of nothing but clear glass. Resting inside of it was a beautiful, young woman.

I approached the box carefully, drawn to the woman inside of it. Her hair was pure black, and though dead, her cheeks still had a rosy color to them. She didn't look dead. She almost seemed as if she were merely in a deep slumber. A sleeping beauty. Her full, red lips against the snow around me grabbed my attention immediately. Never had I seen such naturally red lips. They were like blood.

Without thinking, I pushed the lid of the coffin open. The glass shattered on the forest floor, but

I didn't even notice. Upon closer inspection, I was amazed at how perfectly preserved her body seemed to be. How long had she been out here?

My eyes were drawn to her lips again, and I felt an irresistible pull towards them. What was it the witch said? "You, Prince Oliver, will know your purpose upon looking at her face."

I couldn't stop myself as I dropped to my knees and leaned closer to her face. And then, incredulously, I brushed my lips against hers.

I leapt back. What was I doing? How creepy was I? But there was something weird… Her lips hadn't been cold. They were warm. The girl before me stirred, and I froze. She slowly sat up and stretched her arms, then her eyes flew open. She looked at me with a great look of confusion.

"Where am I?"

Note from the Author

Thank you for taking the time to read my book! I hope you enjoyed it. If you did, spreading the word would be much appreciated! For instance, leaving an Amazon or Goodreads review, or sharing on social media, would make all the difference!

Subscribe to my newsletter and take a look at my website to receive updates, book releases, and so much more!

Newsletter: http://eepurl.com/g-ioqz
Site: https://aleesehughes.com

Be sure to follow me on all social medias:
Instagram: @aleesehughes
Facebook: Aleese Hughes
Twitter: @AleeseHughes

Sneak Peek...

Pumpkins and Princesses

Prologue

Lucinda Brooker was merely the daughter of a poor merchant and never knew any luxury in life, but she always desired it more than anything. That was probably the biggest reason Lucinda loathed her younger sister. The Crown Prince of Greriveth saw Catherine one day in the woods and fell madly in love with her almost immediately. But Lucinda knew that if it had been she who was gathering firewood, she would have been Queen now of the entire Kingdom— not her sister Catherine.

Lucinda was convinced that she was cursed. In addition to the ill-fortune of remaining a poor peasant, her husband died, leaving her alone with two wretched boys. She desperately wanted a daughter to dote on, but no higher power that may be out there thought her deserving. But Catherine had a daughter. Lucinda was not at all pleased to hear the news of Greriveth's Queen bearing twins: a young prince and a beautiful little princess.

As Lucinda snuck through Newvein that night, hood pulled tightly over her thin face, and her limbs trembling from the fright of getting caught, she told herself that Catherine didn't need two children. She would be just as happy with a son to direct all of her attention to. Catherine was Queen, for heaven's sake! What more would she need?

The guards were easy to slip past— Grerivethan soldiers were known for their incredible lack of ambition and skill. A particularly famous story involved the current captain of the guard and a few comrades falling to their knees in terror as bandits looted their bags and pockets with no fight whatsoever.

Lucinda was convinced that if she had been the one in charge of Greriveth instead of her perky, daft sister and her sister's idiotic husband, improvements on the royal guard wouldn't be the only thing to happen. Lucinda knew of so many ways to make the monarchy— and in turn, the kingdom— much more wealthy than it was. She was the daughter of a merchant, and after taking over her father's business, she had learned a lot about money and made her father's merchant trade much more successful than he ever had. Lucinda still wasn't rich by any sense of the word, but she was proud to see the little difference she could make without her overbearing father and husband telling her to keep her mouth shut. And Lucinda knew that if she were on the throne, she would start by creating more trade routes and encouraging all merchants to travel out of Greriveth into the other four kingdoms. And maybe Greriveth could even become wealthy enough for travel across the ocean to Lurid.

Lucinda shook her head. It wasn't the time to get lost in her daydreams. The halls of the castle were unlit and almost spooky as she traversed her way to the nursery. She had an inside tip from a nursing maid as to where she could find the room. The nurse, Giselle Pirone, had watched over Lucinda and Catherine before their father couldn't afford her services anymore. And, out of loyalty, or something, Catherine hired Giselle for her own children.

But Giselle had proven to be more loyal to Lucinda instead of her Queen. Catherine was always the favorite to everyone, being prettier with her golden hair and elegant, willowy figure against Lucinda's white-blonde hair and plump form. Catherine was even referred to as "the one with the kind heart." But Lucinda had a special place in Giselle's heart. Maybe it was because the old nursing maid felt bad for her.

Although she had been given specific directions, the immense size of the building made it harder to navigate than she expected. Lucinda had never been inside the castle, not even for her sister's wedding, or even her and her husband's coronation to King and Queen just ten years after the marriage. She had been invited to both, but Lucinda knew it was merely out of pity. And she wasn't going to give Catherine the satisfaction of coming and showing support for what should have been hers.

After many years of Lucinda ignoring her sister's invitations and being less than friendly when Catherine tried to visit, the Queen got to the point where she gave up on trying to build a good relationship with her sister. Lucinda and Catherine hadn't actually seen or spoken to one another for months.

After maybe ten minutes of frustrating twists and turns, Lucinda finally recognized the hallway that Giselle had described to her. Unlike the others, no portraits were decorating the walls, but the purple carpeting at her feet was thick and expensive. Two doors down to her right, Lucinda found it. She could see why Giselle had said she would know it when she saw it: the white wood of the door was decorated with a delicate, light blue trim around its edges. It definitely looked like a door to a children's room.

Lucinda turned the cold knob slowly and pushed it open, fearing the sound of a creak echoing through the halls, but none came. She sighed in relief and stepped around the door and shut it with a soft click.

"I was getting worried you weren't going to make it."

Lucinda smiled at Giselle. The nurse sat in a plush rocking chair next to the large, bay window behind her. Her graying hair was tied up into a loose bun, and many strands of hair had escaped from it. She looked exhausted as she rocked back and forth with a small, white bundle in her thin arms.

"Is that her?"

Giselle grinned, lighting up her tired eyes. "Do you want to see her?"

Lucinda gingerly stepped over to the old woman, as if frightened of the bundle. As she pulled the blanket down to look upon the little face, tears sprang in Lucinda's eyes. The baby was beautiful with rosy cheeks and a button nose. Her round face turned to look up at Lucinda, and a little smile came from the soft, pink lips.

"Oh," Lucinda breathed. "She's so beautiful."

Giselle's grin grew, deepening the wrinkles in her cheeks. "I think she looks more like you than Catherine."

Lucinda's breath caught as she was reminded of her sister. The nurse seemed to notice.

"I'm sorry," Giselle whispered. "Maybe you should get going."

Giselle slowly stood so as not to wake the Princess and slipped the little bundle into Lucinda's arms. Lucinda felt a shudder of joy run through her veins. The baby gurgled slightly and shifted in her sleep. She really was beautiful.

Lucinda's sons had never looked so exquisite— not even as newborns. They had taken after their all-too-plain father.

"Where's the other one?"

Giselle nodded to the end of the room toward a blue bassinet. "He's sleeping, too."

"What about you?" Lucinda asked. "Will they suspect you?"

The nurse's brown eyes twinkled. "I have quite the story planned."

Lucinda didn't want to know what type of story Giselle had conjured up— she had always been good at the storytelling. Too good.

"What's my best way out of here?" Lucinda said.

Giselle pointed towards the slightly opened door behind them. "Back where you came from. Through the kitchens."

"Thank you."

The two embraced tightly, careful not to squish the child between them, and without a second thought, Lucinda swept away and back through the corridor. She carefully tucked the Princess in the crook of her arm within the folds of her cloak and threw the hood back over her dirty-blonde curls. There still was no one to stop her, and the two guards she saw were slumped to the floor in a drunken slumber. Something really needed to be done about the slothful soldiers.

Lucinda made it to the large, empty kitchens. They were still warm from the use of the ovens for supper that night. The soles of her boots clicked against the tiled floor loudly, and she held her breath until she pushed through the back door and made it back onto the cobbled streets.

Once Lucinda was out of the light of the street lamps and back among the shadows of the trees, she pulled the child from hiding and snuggled the Princess deep into her chest.

Lucinda loved the smell of newborns. The thick hairs atop the child's head tickled her nose as she took in the scent. The baby then stirred awake, but instead of crying, her eyes locked onto Lucinda's own. She gasped, noticing that the child's eyes were a bright hazel like her own.

"She really does look like me," Lucinda whispered into the night. She stroked the baby's soft cheek. "Let's go home, my child."

Want to read more? Get *Pumpkins and Princesses* now!

Map

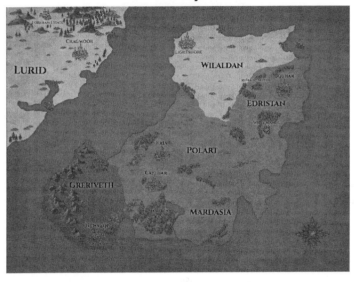

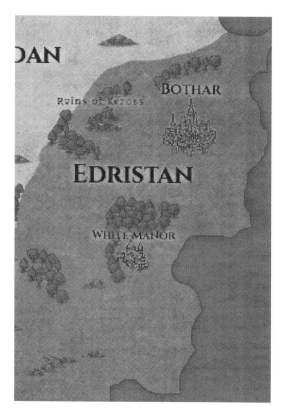

About the Author

Aleese Hughes is many things: a mother and wife, an avid reader, a performer, and an author. Aleese enjoys her time at home with her children and relishes the opportunities to pick up a good book or write one herself.

Having grown up around theater her entire life, Aleese has a natural ability when it comes to charming audiences while on stage. And the same goes for her knack to put words to paper and create stories that people of all ages can read and enjoy.

The fantasy genre is not only her favorite to read, but it is also what she writes, including "The Tales and Princesses Series," and "After the Tales and Princesses- A Set of Novellas."

More by Aleese Hughes

The Tales and Princesses Series

After the Tales and Princesses-
A Set of Novellas